NO ONE
HAS TO
KNOW

CARIN HART

For those who always wanted an obsessed book boyfriend to do anything to keep you...
but who would run the other way if an Officer Burns chose you in real life.

FOREWORD

Thank you for checking out *No One Has To Know*!

This book is a dark romance standalone featuring an obsessed stalker hero, the heroine he takes as his captive, and their whirlwind—and questionable—romance. Burns goes to great lengths to make Angela his, and there are some scenes that push her limits... and more. As such, I want to list out the content warnings here so that prospective readers are informed of what they can expect and decide if this is something they feel comfortable reading.

No One Has To Know includes: stalking, kidnapping, captivity, dub-con/CNC, abuse of power (since the hero is a cop and uses that against her), violence, murder (on and off-page... though it's done to protect/avenge the heroine), mentions of a previous attack and sexual assault of the heroine (happens off-page, years before the book begins), and gun use (including during one steamy scene).

This book is told in dual POV so you can compare Burns's thoughts to his actions and make your own decision on whether he's a hero or not; also, be wary of an unreliable narrator. Either way, he's the perfect hero for Angela—*No One Has To Know* has a HEA ending where the hero and the heroine stay together.

xoxo,
Carin

PROLOGUE

MACE

It's all the fucking daisy's fault.

Not like I need something to blame for my obsession. I don't. I know what I am, and I accept that I would've locked on my angel with or without the flower eventually. Something put her in my path, the perfect prey to my predator. The daisy just sealed the deal.

I'm a bad man. I do what I want—take what I want—and the whole damn world lets me because I have a badge.

It's the perfect disguise, too. As much as cops get shit on, there's a reason so many of us turn out to be garbage. Something about the job calls to a certain type of twisted soul, and I answered the call when I realized it gave me a cover to the darkness inside of me.

People see the uniform first. The gun next. Sometimes the cuffs, or the badge. Rarely do they pay attention to the man instead of the symbol, and that's exactly how I like it.

I'm the one who gets to watch. To observe.

To judge.

Angela Havers thinks I'm a good guy. The friendly cop that patrols outside of Louise's Florals, the small florist shop in the middle of my beat. You wouldn't think flowers would be a big draw in the middle of such a rough-and-tumble neighborhood on the edge of Springfield. You'd be wrong. People seem to appreciate the spot of brightness in the middle of a concrete jungle.

Me? I only give a shit about my pretty little florist.

Seven years my junior, she has an innocence about her that makes her seem even younger. At least until you get a good look at her lovely hazel eyes and realize that they're haunted.

She's seen some shit, but it didn't break her. She's still my angel. Sweet and tender and so utterly delicious, she makes my mouth water for a taste that I can't have unless I want to devour her whole.

She's kind, too. As a cop, I'm used to getting comped. Freebies are part and parcel of having the badge, especially when half the territory you're patrolling is full of criminals, the other made up of the good folk who like the facade that we're here to protect them.

Maybe my fellow cops are. Me? From the moment she shyly flagged me down months ago, offering me a single daisy to brighten my day, I've only ever cared about keeping one soul safe. Of watching her, of learning all her secrets, of obsessing over the moment I could find a way to make her mine.

My angel.

At the very least, she needs the protection. Her innocence blinds her to just how dangerous Springfield can be. I know that all too well. Lowlife crooks scatter around the city like cockroaches, looking up to gang leaders like the dark figure who conducts his business out of the aptly named Devil's Playground on the west side of town.

Meanwhile, Devil himself thinks he rules the streets as easily as he controls his club, his runners, his girls, and his business—and for a favor here and there, and a weekly deposit into my checking account, that's perfectly fine with me.

So long as none of the men in the Sinners Syndicate set their eyes on my woman.

I let it be known that she's under my protection. Anyone who even looks twice knows what's coming for them, and while Lincoln Crewes might be known as the Devil of Springfield, the brawling gangster at least has *some* morals.

I have fucking *none*.

Which is why, after slipping into her apartment building one afternoon months ago, going up to her floor on the pretense that I was answering a fictitious call, I was pleased to see that she had a decent deadbolt lock on it. I'd slit the throat of anyone who thought to hurt my angel, but that wouldn't mean anything if I lost her before I could make her mine.

But while she's got the deadbolt covered, what was the point when she doesn't bother shutting up her windows? It's like a fucking invitation to the worst of us, cop or criminal. Anyone with bad intentions could sneak up the fire escape and let themselves into the sanctuary of her bedroom.

Which is why I spend nearly every night I can climbing into her apartment, standing guard over her as she sleeps.

I find peace in her snuffling snores, and rage in her frequent nightmares.

She's been hurt. My innocent flower has scars she carries deep that only come out when she's sleeping. Her whimpers have me reaching for my gun every goddamn time.

I don't have a name. Can't get one, either, without showing my hand. So, forcing myself calm no matter what it takes, I vow that, if any bastard tries to hurt her again, I'll be there to show him what true justice looks like.

And if I ever get the name of the prick who already did?

He'll live to regret it.

Oh, wait. He *won't*.

I never stay in her shabby studio apartment for long. A few hours—when the worst of the worthless crooks in Springfield are up to no good, and both the Sinners Syndicate and Damien Libellula's corrupt family slink out into the night—before I begrudgingly head back to my empty bed across town; it's not my home, but a place I put my head down between patrols. I have a hunting cabin—my *real* home—up in the hills for when the city life turns me feral and I need some peace before I go rabid, but I haven't gone back since the daisy wilted and died, and I started to worry that the same thing might happen to my precious angel.

The cabin is just too far from her. What would I do if she needed me and I was an hour away? Hell no. I have to keep close because, given how sweet and innocent yet broken she is deep down, the wrong sort of man is attracted to a woman like her.

Ask me how I fucking know.

ONE
ATTEMPTED ROBBERY

MACE

Most of my patrols are daytime shifts.

Too busy on the job, I can't spend as much time watching my angel as I like. Nighttime is ours, but that doesn't mean I don't find her whenever I can.

I do.

And if there's one upside to obsessively stalking a young twenty-five-year-old woman who lives by herself and doesn't put her own safety first? It's how fucking easy it is to discover—and follow—her routine.

Angela never wavers from it. A creature of habit, she goes to work, she goes home, she goes to the corner store... and that's about it.

She has no friends; at least, not locally. Her only family lives four states away. She moved to Springfield about three weeks before she started working in the flower shop. I found her almost immediately, and there's been no other man for her in that time.

No man but me, that is.

She's as much of a loner as I am, another point that proves she's meant for me. I'm drawn to her, like a moth to a flame, addicted to the sight of her light brown hair, her luscious curves, and those wary, guarded hazel eyes. I can find her anywhere, and with her schedules almost as ingrained into me as my own, I know where she is at any given moment.

Whether I'm on duty or not, I stay in uniform whenever Angela has a closing shift. In October, it's pitch black outside when the flower shop shuts up for the evening. The bank where she makes the nightly deposit is five blocks away. I would never risk anything happening to her during those five blocks there, then the ten more blocks to her apartment. I'm there, always watching.

No one sees me. If anything, they notice the cruiser. That's it.

As a cop, most people glance my way, then quickly find something else to occupy their attention. Is it because they're guilty? In my experience, yeah. Nearly everyone's done something they don't want a cop to know about.

Even my precious angel isn't as innocent as she seems.

If anything, that makes me want her *more*.

She doesn't deserve to be stalked and hunted; at least, not by anyone other than me. I only have her safety in mind. The gangly, early twenty-something kid with the knife nervously tucked between his fingers... he just wants the deposit bag Angela has stowed in her purse.

My headlights reflect off of the blade. I was already watching closely when the kid closed the gap between an oblivious Angela and his awkward gait. When his gaze darts around, I recognize him as a local junkie. He goes by the name of Brick, probably because his head's as thick as one.

He thinks he can hurt my angel. He's gotta be a fucking moron to try.

I'm already halfway out of the cruiser when he lunges for her.

Until the day I die, I'll never forget the terror in her scream as Brick goes for the purse strap hanging off of her shoulder with one hand. With the other, he waves the knife wildly.

That was his mistake. He cuts Angela. It might've been a tiny nick on the side of her throat, but when she cries out, hand raising to the spot, I'm already picking out the perfect place in the woods behind my hunting cabin where I'm going to bury him. Then I see the blood smeared on her fingertips as she pulls her hand away, and that seals it.

She freezes. I'm not surprised. With her past, being attacked out on the street for a couple of hundred bucks wouldn't turn her into a fighter. Oh, no. She's easy prey.

She's *mine*.

Poor Brick. Dumb fuck doesn't even know he's dead. Standing there, a complete fool, he's still trying to tug the purse off her suddenly stiff shoulder. Blood trickles down her neck, illuminated by the moonlight. I have half a mind to draw my weapon now, only I'd never forgive myself if I hit her by accident.

The cuffs on my belt jangle. My shoes thud against the ground as I run toward him. At the same time, one of the doors to a still-open shop flings outward. A man steps onto the sidewalk, his expression becoming a shocked stare once it hits him that he's stepped right into the middle of something.

I recognize him. Dean Willows is an actual nice guy who runs this hobby shop near the bank. Another local small business owner, not only does he instantly recognize that this is a robbery in progress, but he knows my angel, too.

And me.

Fuck.

"Officer Burns? Angela? What's going on?"

I'd put money down that it's the 'officer' part that catches Brick's attention.

Swiveling his head, he takes one look at me, then tosses the knife to the ground. His hands free, he shoves Angela away from him before bolting down the street.

No weapon. Damn it. How can I use deadly force when witnesses saw him toss his weapon?

I don't know. Hell if I'm going to let him get away from me, though.

Thanks to Brick's shove, Angela stumbles forward, her path taking her right toward me. For my own sanity, I take a second to steady her. Breathing in her scent—like flowers, fuck, she smells *amazing*—I squeeze her to me. She's okay. A little shaken up. More bloody than I'd like... but she's okay.

Brick won't be.

Dean rushes over to us, forehead on his too-pretty face creased as he tries to make sense of the scene he wandered into.

No time for explanations. I have something to take care of.

"Watch her," I bark at Dean, passing Angela off to him.

It's not what I *want* to do. If I had a partner or backup tonight, I would've rather stayed with her. Since it's just me right now, I have to go after the would-be robber.

I'm a cop. He's a criminal. It's what's expected of me.

And when I'm forced to rein in my murderous fury and stop at tackling him to the sidewalk before roughly cuffing his trembling hands behind his back, I promise myself that this is only the beginning of the payback I'm going to take from him.

He won't get away with harming my angel. Not if I have anything to do with it.

———

To put it bluntly, I became a cop because of everything it could do for me. But because I'm not *that* much of a sociopath, I do believe in justice. So what if it's my own brand of it? As far as I'm concerned, you do the crime, you do the time. You gotta pay for your wrong-doings, and if I have to, I'll be the one to make sure of it.

He scared her. He scared Angela.

I can't forgive that.

Once I have Brick cuffed, I radio for backup. I need to get rid of this trash, and as much as I want nothing more than to kick him to the curb and go back to check that Angela is okay, I need to at least pretend to do this like I'm supposed to.

Then I'll return for her.

I have to. I'd left her with another guy, something

that isn't sitting right with me, and she was shaking when I gave her to him. I need to see her whole and in one piece with my own two eyes, maybe talk to her— but I don't get the chance. By the time Martinez and Pullman finally come by with their cruiser, helping me yank the prick to his feet before shoving him into the backseat, Cassidy is with Angela and Willows, taking their statements.

That's one thing in my favor, I'll admit.

Cassidy's a good cop. Decent. She's got a soft touch when it comes to victims, too, so she's the perfect choice to talk to my pretty little florist. A married mom with three kids of her own, I don't have to worry about Cassidy hitting on Angela; not like Pullman, who's married but will also attempt to fuck anything that moves. I also know she'll assure Angela we're taking the attempted robbery seriously, especially since the perp never got the deposit bag and he dropped his knife when he took off.

It's an open and shut case—or it would be if Angela pressed charges.

I'm not surprised when she hesitates. Still trembling, her voice shaky, her big hazel eyes wide with fear... I know exactly why she's throwing up a wall between herself and the police. She wants to just pretend tonight didn't happen.

I'm happy to oblige.

Even so, I recognize that some things have to be

done by the books. If it was just me, I wouldn't give a shit, but I don't want it getting back to her. So I let Cassidy bring Angela home, while I head down to the police station.

I know better than most that processing can take hours... unless you offer to help a fellow officer along.

Kelly is at the desk. Looks like luck is on my side. A rookie, he's eager to please some of us vets. For some reason, he looks up to us—me especially—and I give him my trademark grin as I approach him.

His eyes light up. "Hey, Mace. What's up?"

"You got a young kid in a holding cell. Goes by Brick?"

"Uh, yeah. Hang on. I've got the paperwork here somewhere." Kelly digs around the desk. This late, processing is a mess. The day cops would've left their reports for the night shift if they didn't finish them, and the night shift would've passed it off to the rookie if they didn't feel like doing it.

Sometimes the bureaucratic nightmare really pisses me off. Others? I'm glad half the job is all about red fucking tape.

Because then it's easy for me to cut right through it.

"Owen 'Brick' Mathison. Yup. Got him right here."

I hold out my hand. Kelly doesn't even think to ask me why I want the folder. He just passes it over.

Unlike Brick, Kelly's a smart kid. He'll go far in the SPD.

"Thanks. I'll take care of it."

"Aw, Mace. You're the fucking best."

I am, aren't I?

Come tomorrow, he won't even remember the case. It'll be one of thirty that had been on his desk. If anything, he'll only recall how I offered to help him. Knowing Angela as well as I do, she won't follow up.

That leaves me more than able to do what I do next.

Heading to holding, I open the cell. Gesturing at Brick, I tell him wordlessly to get off his ass.

If he refused to move, he could've saved himself. Prison's no fun, but it would've been better than what I have planned. He just shows me he's still a dumb fuck. Jumping up, relief warring with suspicion, he immediately slips out of the cell.

Before he can get too far, I clamp my hand on his shoulder. "Come with me."

"Uh, yeah. Sure. Where are we going?"

"Outside."

"What? Really?"

"Yup. Ms. Havers didn't press charges. You're free to go."

He blinks. "I didn't think she would. I... I didn't mean to nick her with the knife. Is she okay?"

No. "She was escorted home. I'd suggest leaving

her be. Of course, if you go anywhere near the victim, you'll be hauled in faster than I chased your sorry ass down."

I know dark. I know violence. I know the desire to hurt—and to have done so. For fuck's sake, any time I peer in the mirror, I see it staring back at me. So when the prick's eyes narrow, a shadow glancing over his long face… I'm not sure who he wants to pay more: me or my angel.

He's pissed. I don't buy the sorry, nervous act. He's pissed he got caught. He got arrested.

Fucker meant to get her with the knife, didn't he?

And that completely seals his fate. He's a threat to Angela. Maybe not tonight. Maybe not tomorrow. Sooner or later, though, he'll go after her if only because he can, and because he recognizes that I chased him once, even if he's getting away now.

I'll do it again, too.

And, that night, when he slinks out of his place against my warning, and he has no idea that I'm off duty—or that I grabbed his address from the paperwork I took from Kelly and followed him home—I prove it to him.

This time, though?

He doesn't get away.

TWO
DINNER WITH DEAN

ANGELA

I t's my first day back at work.

There are only two of us who work at Louise's: me and, well, Louise. Before I moved to Springfield last summer, she ran the shop by herself. It was her baby. Seven days a week, as she watered the flowers, pruning them, dealing with the distributors, growing some of her own, then selling them at such a discount, it's a wonder she can afford to stay open. She only does because her late husband left her with enough cash to run it as a passion project.

That's how I got the job. Flowers... they're my passion, too. In fact, being a botanist has always been my dream job. Then life got in the way, and I thought I'd never get the chance to work with flowers again.

Until I stumbled upon Louise's shop nestled in my new neighborhood. My apartment is kinda crappy, but even the slums cost money. I've been hopping from retail job to retail job since I dropped out of college, moving cities whenever I felt suffocated by the memory of what happened in Fairview five years ago. I can learn a register anywhere, and good customer service skills are worth a lot.

I'm amazing at being who someone else needs me to be.

Louise didn't need an assistant. However, when I asked if she was hiring, we got to talking about flowers. She didn't need an assistant—but she was more than happy to throw a bone to a young woman who was desperately in need of work *and* loved flowers.

She was beside herself when she found out that a local punk tried to rob me for the store's meager deposit two weeks ago. She insisted on giving me two weeks off—with pay—even though I tried to tell her I was fine. I've been scared enough in my life. I didn't want to go back to looking over my shoulder again, especially since I finally feel like I found somewhere to settle down for good.

I might have gotten away with it if Louise didn't see the bandage on my neck. The cut wasn't too deep. I didn't need stitches or anything. A bandage was enough, but the fact that I got cut at all was too much for Louise. She put her tiny foot down, telling me to go home right away.

So I did. And in between filling out my journal and streaming way too much TV on my tablet, I counted down the days until she told me I could come back to work. She also changed the hours so that neither one of us would have to walk to the deposit box alone in the dark.

I tried to tell her that I made it months before anything like that happened. And when it did? One of the local cops was right there, saving the day before Brick could even get the deposit off of me.

Dean, too.

I'd seen Dean in passing before. Most of us who work in specialty shops in downtown Springfield are at least friendly with each other. Louise introduced us about a month ago, when Dean came in to buy his mother flowers for her birthday. He seemed pretty decent. Friendly enough, and a good son.

The night I was almost robbed, he happened to appear right after the cop chased Brick off. Since then, we exchanged numbers at his request. He texted me every day while I was on Louise's imposed vacation, checking in on me. Because of that, he knew exactly when I was returning back to work to give Louise a bit of a well-earned break.

Around lunchtime, he came to visit. I wasn't so

surprised. Honestly, I expected it. He's made one or two mentions of getting to know each other better. He seems to think that it was fate that had us bumping into each other that night. I almost pointed out that it was more Brick shoving me at the police officer who then tucked me against Dean, but... I don't know. That didn't seem fair.

He brought me cookies. Placing them on the counter between us, we steadily make our way through the plate. As the owner of his hobby shop, he can close down for a half an hour to flirt with me. I haven't had a customer all morning and, honestly, maybe I'm more rattled than I thought about being back at work. I think the two weeks off did me more harm than good. I keep seeing Brick lurking outside, only he's not really there when I pay attention.

Almost like he's a ghost haunting me.

Ridiculous, right? It is, but it helps to have a little bit of company.

The cookies are good. Some oatmeal and some chocolate chip. Homemade, he brags, and he should. They taste store-bought.

I kinda think they are.

I don't call him out on his fib. If anything, it's a harmless white lie. Besides, most people aren't completely honest all the time.

I learned that the hard way.

Dean notices that I favor the chocolate chip. I give him points for choosing to snack on the oatmeal from then on. He sprays a few crumbs on the counter as he talks about... trains? It's probably trains. With Dean, that's a safe bet.

I keep an interested expression on my face. In reality, I'm wondering if I should head to the laundromat and do laundry tonight. The forecast calls for rain later in the week. If I don't do it now, good chance I'll run out of clean clothes by then.

Last thing I need is to haul my laundry bags twelve blocks away in the pouring rain...

Someone knocks against the glass. A quick rap-tap-tap with their knuckles.

I give a jolt at the sound. Dean notices. Frowning, he reaches for a chocolate chip cookie. "Look who's stopped by."

I am.

Glancing past Dean, I see the uniform in front of the window. For a split second, my heart stops beating... but then I notice the steely blue eyes and the crooked grin that makes his handsome face even more attractive. He has this hard jaw with just a hint of stubble; it turns him from a boyish man in his early thirties to something that makes my heart rate kick up for a whole other reason.

Officer Burns.

He's the local beat cop, and the same officer who saved me from Brick.

Almost as soon as I first started at the flower shop,

I noticed him. When the weather's nice, he often patrols on foot, lending a comforting presence to the rundown neighborhood. Something about him screams that he's the type of guy you can trust. The type of guy who'll keep you safe.

Who'll do anything to protect you.

A good guy.

I wave at him.

He tips his police cap at me. It covers a head of thick dark hair with just a hint of a curl. The cap lifts, letting loose a strand that falls roguishly forward into his face. His blue eyes twinkle in amusement, and then he's gone.

Dean clears his throat.

I shake my head. "Sorry about that. You were saying..."

Shit. I have no idea what he was saying.

If he can tell, he's good enough not to mention how distracted I am. Instead, he pushes the plate of cookies back toward me. There are two left, both chocolate chip.

"I was just mentioning that cookies might be a good lunch, but I'd love to take you out for dinner. If that's okay with you. I know this great Italian place. It's not too far, and I can pick you up so you don't have to walk."

Hang on—

"You have a car?"

He nods.

Not many people in Springfield do. It's the type of community where we rely on the bus or our feet. Parking is scarce, and gas costs way too much anyway.

So, to be honest, does dinner. I can't tell you the last time I splurged on a meal out that wasn't a knock-off fast food place.

I think about it for a second. When I moved to Springfield, I wasn't sure if I was ready to date again. I thought, maybe, that I might be. When that didn't pan out, I focused on keeping a roof over my head. That's all that mattered to me.

The close shave with Brick was a wake-up call. I'm not owed a damn thing. I could keep putting everything off until tomorrow—or I could try living today.

I don't know if Dean's a good guy. He's a nice guy, though.

Maybe that's just what I need.

"Okay. How about seven?"

THREE
UNDER ARREST

ANGELA

Dinner is... fine.

I don't often get to eat at Mamma Maria's. Only twice since I've lived in Springfield, and one of those times was tonight. It's a little too pricey for me, and if Louise hadn't offered to take me out for my birthday a month ago, I never would've tried it in the first place.

We go dutch. It's going to hurt my pocket a little, not going to lie. I didn't want Dean to get the wrong idea, though. Since Carter, I've been super careful not to let any guy read too much into things I do or say. It fucked me over before, and I never want to be in that situation again.

When I make a move, it'll be obvious. When I want the guy to shoot his shot, I'll make that clear, too.

I like Dean. I think we could be friends. If he's happy not pursuing his attraction to me, I wouldn't mind spending more time with him. We have a few things in common. Neither one of us are Springfield locals—though he's lived here a lot longer than me—and while my fixation is mostly flowers, I've never seen a guy so obsessed with trains. It's actually kind of adorable.

He's cute, too. I'll give him that. With his shaggy, sandy-colored hair and gentle green eyes, there's something almost impish about him. He makes me feel safe. After everything I've been through, I need that.

Do I want to invite him up to my apartment and bang his brains out?

No.

Sorry.

If I'm going to break my years-long celibacy streak, it's going to be with someone I can trust to treat me right. I had enough casual sex in my late teens to last me a lifetime. All that earned me were a couple of trips to the clinic to make sure I didn't catch anything and, later, a bit of a reputation among my classmates.

I thought I could start over in Fairview. Focusing on my studies instead of dating, I made it three years before even keeping my head down wasn't enough to protect me from horny guys who won't take 'no' for an answer...

Dean did. When he invited me back to his place for "coffee", disappointment flashed across his face when I declined, though he didn't push his offer. Instead, mumbling something about having to open his hobby shop early tomorrow, he drove me straight home.

The car ride was a bit awkward. I think it finally hit him that I only agreed to the date because I was grateful to him for being there for me after my whole ordeal with Brick. That, or I thought of him as more of a prospective friend than any kind of lover. Conversing over dinner was a lot easier than the silence that filled the car. Good thing my apartment building is only a few minutes away by car.

I know my instincts about Dean wanting more than I do are right when he drops me off. Nice guys—*good guys*—at least stick around long enough for their dates to get inside safely, right? Especially in a city like Springfield, where I'm recent evidence that it's not a brilliant idea to walk around some neighborhoods after dark.

He doesn't. The second I climb out of his car, it's like he remembered he had another appointment. With a quick honk, he pulls away from the curb, then disappears down the street.

A little bit stunned, I watch him until he makes a

left, vanishing from my sight. Then, with a shake of my head, I turn toward home.

When I see the flashing lights out of the corner of my eye, I wince.

I have to admit, the attempted robbery is still too fresh. Even worse, I called the other day to follow up with pressing charges, and the person I spoke to had no idea what I was talking about. There was no record of it at all.

As for Brick, he's a fixture on the streets. It's how I even knew who he was, and why I was so shocked he would cut me with the knife. Shortly after I moved in, he told off some other guys for harassing me. I threw him a couple of dollars for a smoke. I thought we had some kind of rapport going—until two weeks ago.

I know he got arrested. Officer Burns made sure to stop by my place a couple of days after the attempted robbery to tell me himself. With that charming crooked grin of his, he stood on the porch of my building, and swore that Brick would pay for scaring me.

When he reached out, laying his hand along the side of my throat, casually checking my healing cut... yeah. I should've known better than to accept Dean's date. Not when a dashing, powerful cop like Officer Burns is more my speed.

It's nuts. Up until I met him, I had this... thing about cops. Putting it mildly, I *hated* them. I hated them for not helping me when I needed them. I hated how privileged people can get away with murder—or attempted rape—and the rest of us poor, powerless folk are left to fend for ourselves.

I know it's not just the police. It's the institution as a whole. Everything, from the government down, is set up to screw regular people. I've long accepted that. The only things I can be responsible for are my own actions, and what I manifest in my journal.

I never wrote about a sweet train collector sweeping me off my feet. After tonight's date, I don't think I will.

He left me alone on my porch. With the flashing lights close enough to make me squint against their brightness, there's probably trouble on my doorstep again. Before I get involved, I need to get inside.

I never get the chance.

Brakes squeal. They sound too close.

I refuse to turn around because, in Springfield, you can't get in trouble if you didn't see anything. It was like that in a lot of other places I used to live in. Some day, I hope to find a place where I can live away from these crowded cities. For a while, it seemed like hiding in plain sight was the best thing I could do for my nerves. Lately, I dream of a cozy little place far from the crowds and the danger and the people.

Out of habit, I tap my back pocket. I don't often carry a purse when I'm on the streets. After what happened with Brick, I gave it up completely. Wallet in one pocket, phone in the other, I'm set just like that.

I've got my phone. Not many numbers to call stored inside of it, but it makes me feel better knowing it's there.

A door opens behind me, slamming shut right after. Heavy footsteps come pounding across the asphalt. The jingle jangle of a pair of handcuffs is a big clue that it's a cop.

I scurry toward my building. I've made it maybe three steps before someone yells behind me.

"Stop!"

Though I know the shout isn't for me, I'm nosy. I immediately glance over my shoulder.

I'm shocked by who's there.

"Officer Burns?"

I didn't recognize his voice. Any time we've ever spoken, he sounded so thoughtful. Kind. Friendly. The barking order to 'stop' was so unlike anything I ever heard from him that, even without the command, I would've frozen on the walkway.

It's dark. The nearest lamppost has a broken light. His face is shadowed because of it. The rest of him is silhouetted by the red and blue lights from his haphazardly parked cruiser.

He's marching toward me, hand on the butt of his weapon. "Angela Havers, you're under arrest."

What?

My back is to him. That was my mistake. I didn't turn around. He said 'stop'. I stopped. The second I saw him looming toward me, I wanted to see who it was he was going after. I mean, it couldn't be me, right?

It is.

One of his hands grips my upper arm. He yanks it behind me. I let out of soft cry, half in surprise, and half because it hurt. He's a little more gentle when he goes for my right arm. Still, when he tugs me back against his hard chest, I feel the impact through my whole body.

I never get the chance to scream. Something pricks me and I'm a little distracted by that. I let out a yelp that turns into a gasp when the cold metal of Officer Burns's handcuffs lock around one wrist, then the other in quick succession.

"What are you doing?" I ask when I finally find my voice. "I... I thought you were a good guy."

"I'm the best, angel," he tells me. "That's why you made me do this."

Angel?

Made him do *what*?

Something... something's wrong. My head feels fuzzy. I've got black spots dancing in front of my eyes. If my vision's suddenly going, maybe my hearing is, too.

"Angela," I slur. "My name is Angela."

He knows that. He said my name when he told me I was under arrest.

Only... under arrest for what?

He's got a good grip on my wrists. Thanks to the cuffs, I can't use my hands. I do dig my heels in. If he thinks I'm going to go easily, he's wrong.

Officer Burns makes a *tsk*ing sound that sounds almost... amused. Why the hell is he amused?

What is going on?

"Don't struggle, baby. You'll like me a lot more if you don't struggle."

The words don't make sense. But that tone... I've heard that cajoling tone before. Five years ago, in an unfamiliar bedroom, another man thought he could grab me and make me do whatever he wanted.

"I hate you," I whisper. In my hazy mind, I'm not sure if I'm talking to Officer Burns—or Carter. It doesn't matter. I'm not even sure I said it out loud anyway.

Though I'm almost positive he does say, "You're going to love me," before he shoves me inside of the cop car.

After that, the door slams and everything goes dark.

FOUR
HIS ATTENTION

ANGELA

I'm half awake and already I can sense that something... something's not right.

My head is woozy, with a ton of pressure. It feels full, like someone grabbed a wad of cotton balls and shoved it between my ears. My mouth, too. It's so dry that I'm super thirsty, and it feels as though someone is stabbing me in the back of my throat with a pointed stick, it's that pinchy and painful.

My eyes still closed, clinging to the last vestiges of sleep, I lift my hand to rub my throat. Only... my arm is heavy. Not only that, but when I move one hand, the other moves, like they're connected.

Connected...

Cuffs.

My eyes spring open at the same time as I bolt up. It would've been easier if I had the use of both of my hands but I don't. Just like I thought, my hands are cuffed together with a pair of heavy-duty, metallic handcuffs. I fall back, staring up at an unfamiliar ceiling as I struggle to figure out what the hell is going on.

Okay. Calm down, Ang. Think... it's rough, with my head spinning, my heart racing, but I try.

Last night... okay. The last thing I remember is that cop coming after me. I was on a date with Dean. I was just heading home after dinner, hoping I could get away without having to give him a kiss goodnight, and then... I was arrested?

I was there, and it still doesn't make sense. The cop clapped a pair of handcuffs on me after announcing I was under arrest. My hands were jerked behind my back, the metal of the cuffs biting into my wrists, as he forced my head to duck so that he could shove me into the back of his cop car.

He said something, too. I don't remember what, just that he said something and I'm pretty sure it wasn't an answer to what I had done to deserve being put in cuffs.

They were behind me last night. I remember that part vividly. Now? They're in front of me, and when I pull myself up into a seated position and hear another jingle jangle, I realize that my hands aren't the only part of me contained.

I have a shackle on my ankle, and a length of chain disappearing off the edge of the small bed I'm lying on.

What the—

At first glimpse, it almost seems like a prison cell. Not that I have any firsthand experience beyond what I've seen on television, but the room I'm in is dark, musty, and cool. There's one window, high over my head on the wall at my back; it's covered in a set of thick metal bars. A low wooden table—like a mockery of a coffee table in some rich guy's house—is in the middle of the space. It's holding a thick book with a dark green cover.

But the more I look around, the more I have to admit it isn't. I still don't have any idea where I am, though there's a set of stairs along the wall opposite me that lead somewhere; that, plus the angle of the weak light streaming down from the barred window, makes me think I'm underground. I see a door I can't get to, thanks to the chain on my leg, and there's a fridge about half the size of the one in my apartment humming away merrily.

It's the only sound I hear. Well, that, and the sound of my quickened breath as I begin to panic.

Scooting down to the edge of the narrow bed, I use my cuffed hands to grab the chain. A quick tug reveals that it's stuck. Probably connected to the bed frame since it makes a creaky, jerking sound when I tug again and again.

I'm trapped. Terror wells up inside of me. I quickly shove it down. It won't help me figure out how I got into this mess. I need a level head.

I need to *think*.

Dropping the chain, I go for my pockets. I'm still wearing the same jeans and sweater I had on last night when I went out with Dean. During my look around before, I didn't notice my purse anywhere, but I have a habit of leaving my phone in my back pocket.

It's not easy. I only have so much reach with my hands in the cuffs, and the chain makes it so that I can't even get off the bed. My only hope is to flop on my side and move a bit like a fish out of water, trying to slap one pocket, then the next, searching for my phone.

It would've been worth it if I had it on me—but I don't. Whoever trapped me down here wasn't considerate enough to leave me with some way to call for help.

"Damn it!"

Crap. That was really loud. And since I could be in a lot of trouble, I probably don't want to alert anyone to the fact that I'm awake. Not until I can get a better handle on what exactly is going on.

I'm too late. Within seconds of my outburst, I hear

a door squeak open. I swallow my gasp, my heart pounding even louder as someone starts walking down the stairs right as I force myself to sit up again.

I see shiny shoes first, followed by legs enclosed in pressed black pants. The swagger screams *male*; the uniform shouts *cop*. Makes sense, since the last thing I remember is getting arrested, but when he appears at the bottom of the stairs, I get the feeling that nothing is what it seems at all.

It's only cemented when a wicked grin crosses his devilishly handsome face.

"You wanted my attention, angel. Well, now you have it."

My mouth falls open. Logically, it also makes sense that he's responsible for this. He was the last person I saw before I woke up down here, but he's... he's a *cop*. He's supposed to be the good guy. And, sure, my previous experiences with the police work against him, but Burns... he was a nice guy. He saved me from being robbed, and he came by the flower shop to make sure I was doing okay.

But that's logic. Instinct tells me something different—and I don't know which one is right.

"Officer Burns? What... what's going on?"

He's supposed to be the good guy, but if he is, why is my impression of him so devilish? It only grows when his grin widens before he clicks his tongue, shaking his head slowly. With an easy, casual grace, he moves a little closer, crossing his arms over his brawny chest when he gets halfway to me.

"Angela, Angela, Angela... you should've known better."

I'm not surprised he knows my name. Since he took over the patrol outside of Louise's, we've been friendly enough. He was Burns, and I was Angela, though sometimes he would tease and ask me what an angel like me was doing in a rough neighborhood like Springfield. It always seemed like a play on my name and I never thought twice.

Now I am.

I still don't get it. Known better? Know better about *what*? "Me? Why? What did I do?"

He arrested me. I still don't know why, only that Dean had just driven off when Officer Burns suddenly appeared. Shouldn't I be down at the SPD station if I really did something wrong? Because I'm pretty sure this isn't it—

—and Burns's unexpected answer seals it.

"What did you do? You tried to give yourself away to another man. You're not allowed. That pussy is *mine*."

I blink.

What?

I take a deep breath. I can't help it. The second I realize that this was no accident, that somehow I'm cuffed to a tiny bed in a chilly, musty room with

Officer Burns talking about my vagina belonging to him, I only have one thought left: *scream.*

I barely get out the beginning of a blood-curdling yell before he's right there, bending over me as he grips my jaw in a bruising hold. He squeezes, the pain powerful enough to strangle the sound mid-scream. I choke, especially when he forces my teeth to click close.

He doesn't squeeze for long. The moment my scream dies, he releases his grip. I get the feeling he didn't want to hurt me, but he also isn't going to stand there and let me scream bloody murder.

Especially when he angles my chin so that I'm forced to meet the steely look in his dark blue eyes as he says, "Don't scream again. If you scream, I'll have to gag you. But it won't be with material."

Letting go of my face completely, he rises up until he's standing, then drops his hand to his crotch. He's wearing his police uniform, but the pants don't have enough give to hide the obvious bulge he's sporting.

"I have something that fits perfectly in your mouth," he adds, leaving no doubt what he means, "and when you scream again, I swear we'll both like it."

Not so sure I agree with that last part, but it doesn't matter, does it? His meaning is perfectly clear: no screaming or else I'll be choking on his dick instead.

Got it. As if the 'pussy' comment didn't make it

perfectly clear, sex is on his mind. He can keep it there, just like he can keep his dick in his pants.

My mouth is still closed from how he forced it shut. Refusing to unscrew my jaw—if only because I can just see him taking that as permission to do whatever the hell he wants to me—I press my lips firmly together and give him a jerky nod.

"Good girl."

Okay. The way he purrs the praising comment like that? I can't help the sound that escapes me. It's not a scream, but a whimper that seems to echo around the quiet basement.

Damn it. I wish I could've been silent. Actually, no. I wish I could be defiant and dare him to do it. After all, this isn't some kind of accident. Bringing me to this musty room, cuffing me to a bed, threatening to fuck me... Burns has a motive that I'm trying desperately to ignore.

Because, deep down, I know why I'm here. I know what he wants from me.

No. What he *expects* from me. And there's a pretty good reason why he's chained me to this tiny cot, hidden away like this.

Mine...

FIVE
THE DAISY

ANGELA

I whimper again, and for good measure, I tremble.

He smiles at me, savoring my reaction. Almost like he's enjoying my fear.

Like it turns him on—and maybe it does. His pointer finger is lazily stroking alongside the noticeable bulge, an obvious reminder of his earlier threat.

"You don't know what that sound does to me... you will, just not yet. Let's get this over with first. See, I actually *do* want you to scream. Especially when I'm fucking you... oh, angel, I can't *wait* to hear you shout my name. I'll own your screams, just like I own you— but if you think it's going to save you from me..."

Burns goes for the gun on his hip, unsnapping the holster in a practiced move. Before I have any idea what he's doing, he yanks it from its holster, aims, and fires.

It's a crack of lightning, an explosion that's way too fucking close to me. The bullet whizzes a few feet before slamming into the cinder block wall. It explodes in a cloud of dust.

Deafened from the sound of the shot, I scream though I can't hear it. My fight or flight reflex kicks in, and all I want to do is get away from him. I jump up from the cot, nearly falling flat on my face when I remember too late that my leg is still attached to a chain. Luckily, it's long enough that I can take a few steps away from the cot to satisfy my urge to bolt without doing anything more than stumble.

Burns looks pleased with himself as he lowers the gun.

"I have neighbors. If they didn't hear that, they won't hear you." His eyes brighten. "So those screams are mine alone. But, please. Feel free to shout if you'd like. The sooner you learn I don't make threats, the better." With his other hand, he reaches for his pants. His pointer finger flicks open the top button. "Give me a reason to prove I don't make threats. I only make promises."

I gasp. "You... you can't do this!"

"I'm a cop, angel. I can do any fucking thing I want. And, now that you're here with me, that includes you."

Sex again.

"Why do you keep calling me that? 'Angel'? My name is Angela."

It's a ridiculous deflection. Who cares what he calls me? That's nothing compared to what he has in mind for me, but since I can't even think about Burns nabbing me because he wants to get laid, I focus on the name thing.

And I try not to whimper again when he actually answers me.

"Because, at first, you saved me from the dark thoughts." From the way his gaze roves over me, I can guess what those thoughts are about. "But then they just got darker. I had to take you. I had to make you mine, and the only way to do that was to *make you mine*. Lover... captive... prisoner. It doesn't matter to me what you are so long as I can claim you. You belong to me, and that means you belong *with* me—locked up or not."

My legs go weak. Hearing him confess that he took me for his own pleasure, that he's never going to let me go... I think that broke me. No. Being kidnapped—*that* broke me. The rest of me is just catching up to the shocks and revelations that have been thrown my way since I had the misfortune to wake up.

I manage to make it back to the cot before my legs can't hold my weight anymore. Landing on the edge of the mattress, Burns takes it as a sign that I'm accepting everything he's done to me.

"Good. I want you to be comfortable. That book"—he points at the table—"is yours. If you get hungry, the fridge is yours, too. This is your room." Burns pauses, then adds, "At least, until you beg me to join mine, it is."

My emotions are all over the place. I'm scared, worried, and confused—and those are just the emotions I can recognize. It's hard for me to turn off the attraction to the friendly cop I've nursed these last few months, and I almost want to search corners for hidden cameras because this has got to be a big joke, right? This can't really be happening to me...

Only... it is. The truth of it is in his smirk, and the easy way he fired that gun at the wall. The room stinks of gunfire, the cinder block dust settling near the fridge. My ears are still ringing, too. So, yeah. No denying that this is all real.

You know what isn't? His delusion that all he has to do is lock me in his basement and I'll fall back on the cot, legs spread, and give him everything his sick mind thinks he deserves—including me willingly going along with this.

I'm not brave. After what happened in Fairview, I hid for a long time. I never went back to FU, and it took plenty of therapy to even get me to walk alone at night.

My fears all came rushing back when I got jumped for the nighttime drop. I was able to push past it easier this time because I've become a freaking master of denial.

I could lie to myself, and believe every single word spilling from my lips.

There's something about Burns, though. I should be terrified. I should be pissing myself in fright, begging for my freedom, offering him anything so that he'll bring me back to Springfield and we can forget this. Chalking it up to a break from sanity, he could go back on patrol, I could go back to Louise's, and we could forget this ever happened.

I know that's not going to happen. Everything, from the possessive way he handled me to the dare in his stance as he stands there, gun hanging lightly from his grip... he's not backing down.

I'm not, either.

I have no clue where the nerve comes from, but before I lose it, I jut out my chin and snap, "I'll never want to stay with you!"

For a moment, my words echo almost as loudly as the gunshot, though he doesn't react. Just the opposite, actually. He's perfectly still, his expression unreadable as he continues to stare at me.

That makes it so much worse.

Heart racing, pulse pounding, I immediately regret snapping at him. He's dangerous. *Unstable.* Defying him could end up being a death sentence, and I don't know what came over me.

Or him.

Burns moves. Quicker than I would've given him credit for, he crosses the space between us. Before I know it, he's looming in front of me. There's nowhere for me to go as his hand goes to my throat, a collar that forces my head back and my lips to part on a sudden gasp as he pulls me to my feet.

Swooping down, he kisses me fiercely while gently squeezing my neck. It's a claiming kiss, possessive and invasive at the same time. He sucks my tongue into his mouth, before dipping his into mine, stroking my tongue, clashing our teeth together. I'm powerless to stop him, and I don't even try.

When he's finally done, he pulls back, dark blue eyes gleaming. His voice is a throaty rasp as he says, "Fuck me, angel, but your lies taste *delicious*."

I'm stunned for a moment before realization sets in. He's still holding onto me with such a possessive grip that I don't even think. I just act, shoving him in the chest.

My own is heaving. Panicked breaths fill my lungs again, coming out in shallow gasps. The fact that I can taste Burns in my mouth makes this so much worse. For all his threats, I never thought he'd just kiss me like that, and my only thought is putting space between us.

To my surprise, he steps away from me. I fool myself into thinking I saw a flash of concern skitter across his face as I use my cuffed hands to clutch my boob.

It hurts. I wince. It hits me just then that there's been a mild ache coming from that spot since I got up. The woozy feeling in my head—drugs, I bet, or some kind of sedative—caused a disconnect. I didn't realize that it stung so bad until his forearm hit my boob as he formed a collar with his hand.

"You okay, angel?"

Depends. The more I'm focusing on it, the more it feels like I've been burned.

He's a persistent bastard. "What's the matter? Something wrong?"

The way he says that... he did something. I don't know what. I could guess why, but Burns... he did something.

"What did you do to me?"

"Gonna have to be a bit more specific there if you want me to answer that. Go on. Your screams are mine, but so is your curiosity. Don't be afraid to ask questions. I'll tell you whatever you want to know."

That's the problem. Consider me an ostrich who prefers to stick her head in the sand, but I don't want to know. I don't want to hear his answers, or make any sense of this madness. I just want to fall asleep, wake up, and be back in my apartment.

That's not going to happen, though. So, instead, I pat my tit, squealing when the dull ache becomes a stinging sensation that I can't ignore.

Raising my cuffed hands, I pull on my collar—and then shriek.

"Ah. You're just noticing my little gift to you."

Little gift. Little. Gift.

Little gift?

It's a fucking tattoo. I went to bed without any, and now I have a tattoo at the height of my left boob.

I can't really read what the black ink says. I think there are a few letters, maybe some numbers, but from my angle, they're upside down. Plus there's some kind of shiny ointment smeared over it, with a clear bandage covering that makes it hard to decipher.

I can't peel off the bandage. Not without taking off my shirt, and definitely not while I have handcuffs on. Instead, I tug my sweater down enough that I can kinda see what it says.

My stomach goes tight. "'Burns'?" I read. "It's... it's your name?"

"And my badge number. In case you had any doubt you're mine, don't. I put my mark on you. The first woman who earned it," he adds, answering a question I never would've thought to ask, "and the only one."

I have so many questions. My biggest one is 'why', of course, though I don't think I'm in the right state of mind to hear his answer to that. Instead, I demand, "How?"

It's high enough that I want to pretend he didn't get a look at my boob while I was being branded with his name. As if I believe that. Whatever he did to put me to sleep, that made me so groggy when I woke up... I slept through a fucking tattoo. What else could I have slept through?

As my world is spiraling around me, Burns grins again.

It's that charming grin of his I've seen countless times before, never thinking anything of it other than —damn it—it was so effortlessly sexy. So deceptively innocent, too, with just a hint of a dare lingering around the corner of his mouth.

"I did it myself," he says. "In case you ever forget who you belong to, look to your heart. Figure, your name is already etched on mine. Only fair that you wear mine on yours... or as close to it as I could get. But just because you're the first woman I decorated, you're not the only one I've left my mark on."

Before I can ask what he means by that, he rolls up his sleeve. His forearms are brawny and thick, with a single tattoo inked just below the crook of his elbow.

It's a daisy. The big, bad cop has a dainty daisy tattooed on his skin.

I love flowers. I've spent my whole life fascinated by them, and when I would think about getting a tattoo of my own, I could never narrow down what kind of flower I would want to carry around on my skin permanently.

But Burns did—and he chose a *daisy.*

One of my favorites.

I don't know what to say. I'm sure he's showing me the tattoo for a reason, though I can't get past the fact that he inked me while I was unconscious. Unlike his daisy, there's no ambiguous meaning for the letters and numbers on my chest. He marked me. *Branded* me.

That pussy is mine...

So, my obviously insane captor thinks, is the rest of me.

SIX

FOREVER, BASICALLY

MACE

I t takes every ounce of willpower I have to leave Angela alone so I can head back to Springfield for my shift, especially after the kiss.

I'd planned on taking it slow. Knowing I have her in my possession should've been enough for now. And I believed that up until the moment she tried to tell me that she'll never stay with me.

I know her. I know her thoughts. I know her secret desires. I know what gets her hot at night, what makes that pussy grow wet, and I'm going to give her everything she wants. She might not understand that I'm doing this all for her *now*, but she will. I just have to wait.

Pity patience has never been one of my strong points.

So I took her mouth.

I had to get inside of her, one way or another, to brand her as effectively as I did when I marked her with my name and my badge number.

Before Angela, being a cop was all I was. It was my identity, the reason I existed through the drudgery of day-to-day life. It's still a big part of what I am, though my pretty little florist has wormed her way beneath the armor, beneath the uniform, owning me completely from the moment she did something so sweet and innocent as giving me a fresh daisy.

Should I have shown her my own tattoo? Maybe not. I'm still proud of it. And, okay, I wanted her to ask about it, too.

I want her to *know*.

At the station, my fellow cops know me as the patrolman with the gun—tattoo gun, that is. It's something I picked up when I was in my late teens. Something about getting beauty out of pain spoke to a young Mace, and I liked watching the blood welling up on their skin as I got away with stabbing people hundreds of times. When they yelped, I grinned. Knowing I own a piece of everyone I've inked is a heady thought, too.

I don't do pretty designs. It's just not my style. Like the lines scrawled on the height of my angel's creamy, gorgeous breast, I do names, numbers, and a pretty decent shield. Cop ink. I never even marked my body —my fucking temple—until I felt the urge to carry a reminder of my angel on me everywhere I went.

That daisy means everything to me. Once I have my ring on her finger and her ass in my bed where it belongs, I plan on having her scrawl her name on my heart. I want it in her handwriting, just like I want her to be the one to witness how pain and pleasure go hand in hand.

But that's not today. I have to wait.

For my angel, I will.

I've already been more impulsive than I should have been. When I saw her leaving her apartment building last night, wearing the sweater that shows off her tits, and the jeans that highlight the curve of her ass... those were date clothes.

When the car pulled up in front of her apartment and I saw Willows in the driver's seat? I knew exactly who thought they could steal my angel from me.

I was off duty, looking forward to the few hours I could be with Angela. When I could assure myself that she was doing fine.

Instead, it turned into a stake-out. I followed them to Mamma Maria's, nabbing a table not too far from where they were seated.

He got eggplant parmigiana. My angel ordered ravioli.

They shared wine.

Fucker wanted to get her drunk.

That did it. No way in hell was I going to stand there and watch as another man made moves on my girl.

She never knew I was there. That's the beauty of the badge. Without it, I'm not Officer Burns. I'm Mace —but Angela hasn't met him yet. She only knows the cop.

Her hero.

I saved her again tonight. I'm not sure she'll ever see it that way. I mean, I went back to my place, traded my street clothes for my uniform, and grabbed the sedative I prepared because—shit—I knew this day was coming. I waited until Willows dropped her off, then made a big display of arresting her so that, in case anyone was watching, they wouldn't start asking questions when Angela disappeared.

The drugs I got from Crewes worked fast. Devil knew better to ask what one of the boys in blue wanted with a sedative like that, but he got it for me— no questions asked, no questions answered, just like the way we always do business. Jabbing her with the needle as gently as I could, she was out by the time I had her in the back seat of the cruiser.

She had no idea I made a quick trip up to her bedroom, or that I rolled her for her phone. Angela was unconscious the entire trip up to the hills, and when I brought her to the finished basement of the hunting cabin where I plan on keeping her until she promises that she'll never let another soul come between us.

Especially not another guy.

I'm a bad man. I do bad things.

I always have a reason, though. A justification. Even if only to myself, there's a method to my madness.

And, in time, my angel will understand that.

Now that she's awake and aware that I'm not about to let her get away from me, I decide to show her that I'm not the monster she obviously thinks that I am. I unlock the shackle around her ankle and coil up the chain keeping her tethered to the cot. I make sure to point out the closed door, showing her the basic toilet and shower stall that came with the finished basement. When I bought the hunting cabin, it intrigued me, almost as though I knew the darkness inside of me would one day lead me to needing a place to keep my pretty little angel.

For leverage, I leave the cuffs on her. She'll still be able to use the bathroom or get a snack from the refrigerator while wearing them. For now, she's my personal prisoner in a secret cell. The handcuffs aren't a subtle way to hammer that message home, but I don't plan on forcing her to keep them on for long. Just until she earns a little more freedom from me.

I'm not that much of a monster—but I won't deny what I am.

Even better, I don't have to hide around her. Not Angela Havers. By the time I've fully claimed her, my angel will know every inch of me the same way I will her. I got a head start, of course, but she just got a crash course on who Mason Burns is. Not just Officer Burns, with his badge and his gun and his pledge to "protect and serve", but Mace the man.

Her man.

Taking her last night was impulsive. I'm still in the middle of my five-on, two-off patrol, so I'm due in to work by four. The sedative I gave her wore off by noon, just like I figured. Since my cabin in the hills is an hour's drive out of Springfield, I wanted to make sure I had the chance to check on her before I headed in to work. I've got two more shifts, then two full days I can spend with her.

The hours drag. All I want to do is return to her, but I can't let anyone suspect that I stole her.

Last night, after I got her settled in and prepped her for her mark, I covered my tracks. In the corner of Springfield where Angela lives, cops are a pretty usual sight; so is someone getting arrested on their doorstep. If anyone saw what went down, they probably developed temporary blindness so I'm not worried about that.

The prick sniffing around her was a bit more of an

issue. Her boss, Louise, too. Good thing I got her phone off of her. A couple of texts later, and that was taken care of.

Just in case, I do my beat, parking my cruiser along the main, strolling around like I usually do. I nod at the shop-workers, decline a free pastry from the girl waitressing at the cafe I pass every day, and offer Louise a wave when I see the older woman manning the counter in the flower shop.

That's right. It's a regular, ordinary day. No one knows that my whole world has changed, and that none of them will ever see Angela again.

She's mine. No matter what I have to do, no matter how I have to convince her... she's mine, and the sooner she accepts that, the better.

I DON'T EVEN STOP TO CHANGE WHEN I RETURN TO THE cabin. Parking my cruiser on the dirt path next to it, I let myself inside, then head straight for the basement.

It's dark. Well past nine o'clock by now, the sun set a couple of hours ago. There's a single lamp in the basement, leaving a mellow yellow light washing over the space. It's more than enough for me to find Angela curled up on the cot, chin dipped to her chest as if trying to hide from my searching gaze.

I give her a moment to get used to my presence.

Pushing her too hard will only make it so that I have to keep her down here longer. Neither one of us wants that. So, while she studiously ignores me, I look around the room.

The garbage pail by the fridge is knocked on its side. Something tells me she got up and kicked it in a fit of frustration, then left it where it fell. The thick book on flowers I bought for her is moved just enough from the center of the table that I'm sure she at least looked at it.

Score one for Mace.

The door to the bathroom is closed. Since the basement doesn't stink like piss, she must've used it instead of spitefully soiling the cot like I might have done if I were in her shoes. Good. She's not happy, but she's adjusting to being my prisoner better than I could've hoped.

Nodding in approval, I move over to the pail. I pick it up, growing when I see there's nothing inside of it. No wrappers. No bottle of water.

I check the fridge. It hasn't been disturbed. It's exactly as fully stocked as I left it earlier this afternoon —which means that she got her spite out in a whole other way.

Glancing over my shoulder, I ask, "Did you eat?"

She doesn't answer.

I swallow the rush of anger welling up inside of me. She might think she's only hurting herself by refusing to take care of herself. She's wrong. I brought Angela here. I will take care of her.

No matter what.

Reaching into the fridge, I grab a bottle of water and a candy bar. Not the healthiest choice, but it's her favorite, and she probably needs the hit of sugar right now. I tear off the wrapper, toss it in the garbage pail, then stalk over to Angela.

She's still got her cheek pressed to the cot, refusing to meet my gaze.

Yeah. That's not going to work for me.

"Sit up."

She shakes her head.

I grit my teeth. The chocolate is melting in my hand, and she's not the only one who needs to eat. "Fine. Either you sit up yourself, or you sit on my lap. Your choice."

I leave no room for her to misunderstand me. As though remembering how I told her that I don't make threats, only promises, she doesn't try me. Without a word, she starts to rise up into a sitting position.

It's hard, given the cuffs she's still wearing. Taking pity on her, I set the bottle of water on the cement floor, then hook my hand under her armpit so that I can lift her the rest of the way up. She tried, at least, and I reward her by shoving the candy bar right in front of her pouty lips.

"Bite."

She does.

"Attagirl." I wait for her to chew and swallow, then say, "Again."

I don't stop until she's eaten the entire candy bar. That done, I uncap the water bottle. I have the urge to lick the chocolate from her lips myself. Maybe if she didn't look so haunted, I would. Instead, I make her drink. I don't let her stop until she's drunk at least half of the bottle.

I recap the bottle, dropping it to the floor, then join her on the cot. I can tell she wants to move away from me, though she doesn't dare.

Ah. She's learning.

"When I'm home, we eat together. But when I'm on duty, I expect you to feed yourself. If there's something you want that I don't have, tell me. I'll make sure you have it. You will eat, though. I won't let anyone think I can't take care of my angel. You understand me?"

She nods slowly.

Not good enough. "I said, do you understand me?"

"I—yes, but... please, Officer Burns. You have to see... this is wrong, right? You can't just keep me down here."

"Of course, I can."

"No. Listen to me... please. I have a job. You know that. Louise's... I already missed today. She'll be worried about me, and I can't afford to lose my job."

I expected her to go this route. Luckily, I'm prepared.

"You don't have that job anymore. You quit."

She recoils. "What?"

"Well, I quit for you, but Louise thinks you're the one who sent the text, so, yeah. You quit."

"Sent the... you used my phone?"

That's not all I did with it. Like a master observing the chessboard, planning his next moves, I studied every damn thing I could find in her phone to give me the advantage. "Yup. She understands, by the way. After you were nearly robbed... you can go back anytime you want. You won't, of course. As mine, you'll never have to work again."

Her pretty hazel eyes dip down. She nibbles on her bottom lip, thinking hard.

She lifts her chin. "My apartment—"

Nice try, angel.

"I already paid the rent." Next month's, too. Angela will want her belongings, and I have fond memories of that place. She'll never live there again, but I've spent many nights fantasizing about taking her up against the window, showing all of Springfield—my territory —who she belongs to. Once I don't have to keep her against her will, I want to do just that... and I fucking hope Dean Willows gets a front row seat to what he can never have. "For as long as you're with me, you don't have to worry about having a roof over your head."

So... forever, basically.

She's grasping at straws now as she blurts out, "My parents. My mom... she'll go nuts if she doesn't hear from me."

I took care of that, too. "You let her know you're taking a well-deserved vacation." I pause, then add, "With your new man."

I'm more than that. I'm her forever—just like she's mine—and it's time her family knows that. So what if Gina Havers found out before her daughter? I can't have anyone wondering why my angel's disappeared until I'm ready to share her with the rest of the world again.

Which, depending on how well she takes to being mine, might be *never*.

I've stumped her on my last retort. Smart girl, she's quickly learning that I have an answer for fucking everything.

Still, watching her closely, I can just about see the gears whirring in that brain of hers before she finally asks, "But... why? Why here? Why *me*?"

I've been waiting for this question. Too bad she's not ready for the real answer. Angela is still clinging to this idea that I'm doing this to hurt her or some ridiculous shit like that. Until she understands just how devoted I am, I can't let her see the depths that I'm willing to go to keep her.

So, instead of telling her the truth, I tell her *a* truth.

"Why? I brought you home with me because I wanted to see this hair spilled on my pillow." I pick up a strand of the light brown mass of wavy hair flattened from her drugged sleep, tucking it behind her ear. "Your hair is so fucking pretty."

Angela's expression is mixed. There's fear there— as unavoidable as it is—and suspicion, which I also get. She's not used to a gentle touch, and I'm not any better. I couldn't help it, though. When she screamed earlier this afternoon... when she acted like being here with me wasn't what she wanted... I was rougher than I should've been.

I make up for it now with a soft stroke under her chin as I tilt her head back, forcing her to meet my gaze as I tell her honestly, "It'll be even prettier once I fuck it wild."

SEVEN
PETTING

ANGELA

His touch is so gentle.

His possessive words? They're the exact opposite.

All day long I obsessed over what I was doing here. Before he left me to go to work, Burns gave me the use of my legs. After he was gone, I immediately ran up the stairs, checking to see if I was locked in. Of course I was. He went through a lot of trouble to take me, to put me in this basement cell of his, and he wasn't going to risk me escaping so soon.

I'm not tall enough to reach the high window. Even if I could, the bars make it useless. The gaps between them are so tiny, I could maybe reach a couple of fingers through—*maybe*. No one can see me, no one can hear me, and I was left alone in the room with my thoughts, the humming fridge, and the book.

A Gardener's Guide to Botany.

How the hell did he know? Just because I worked in a florist shop didn't mean that I was into his flowers. I *am*—I always wanted to be a botanist—but *how did he know?*

I couldn't look at it. Just like I couldn't bring myself to eat any of his food. The second I got curious enough to pop the door open on the fridge and saw it was full of things I actually liked, I was too freaked out to even have any.

He made me eat the candy bar. Big mistake. My stomach is roiling now with the realization that my suspicions are right. For whatever reason Burns chose me, he wants sex.

No. He wants to *fuck* me.

"I... you can't."

"Can't I?" His gaze dips down to his crotch, a wicked smile curving his lips. "If you welcomed me right now, I'd show you just how wrong you are."

Without meaning to, I follow the path of his steely blue eyes. The cut of his uniform pants does little to hide the erection he's sporting behind them. "That's not what I meant."

"It's not. Then do tell, angel."

He's mocking me. Teasing me. He can stroke me

gently, then say something filthy, leaving me off balance though he's made his intentions clear.

If he knows anything about me at all, he'd know that taking my choice away... I'll never forgive him. I'll never get over it.

Like what happened to Carter, it'll break me. Only, with Burns, because I trusted him—because I desperately wanted to trust his badge—it would shatter me.

My breath catches in my throat. I promised myself earlier that I wouldn't let him see how much being his prisoner affected me. He's looking for a reaction. I refused to give him one—until now.

"You wouldn't..."

That's all I can get out before the emotions get to be too much. I choke, my hands trembling. I try to cover it up by clutching my jeans, digging my nails into the denim. No use. He sees it.

He sees fucking *everything*.

Burns lays his calloused palm over the top of my right hand.

"I won't force you. When I take you... when I make you mine, Angela, you'll be begging me to fuck you."

I stare at the top of his hand. His knuckles are thick knobs, a few thin scars crisscrossing over the flat part of his skin. "You keep saying that."

"What?"

"That I'm yours."

"Because I mean it."

Daring a look up at him, I scoff. "Until you get bored with me. What happens then?"

"Nothing because that'll never happen. I love you, angel."

Impossible. "You can't. You don't know me. Not really."

"Oh?" Instead of looking annoyed, he seems amused. "You sleep with a knife under your pillow. You did that before the robbery so I know you have past trauma. You make sure your doors are locked, but you forget about the window sometimes. Lucky for me, or I'd have a harder time getting inside your apartment."

I blink. "You've never been in my apartment."

"Oh?" Burns raises his eyebrow. "Let me prove it." Using his pointer finger, he draws a square in the air in front of him. "Your bedroom. Bed's on this side. You've got a desk over here, and an old chair that's missing one of its wheels. It doesn't wobble that much for you because you rarely sit in it... you prefer to journal in your bed... but I brought oil with me one night so I didn't wake you up when it squeaked. See, I weigh more than you, angel, and as much as I don't mind standing over you to watch you sleep, I'm on my feet all day. A man's gotta sit sometimes."

Most of everything he says to me is white noise. Background fodder. I'm barely listening from the moment he mentions my journal.

My heart lodges in my throat. "How do you know about my journal?" Terror wells up, replacing the panic. "Did you read it?"

"Does it matter?"

"Yes."

He takes my chin gingerly in his hand. "Get used to disappointment. When you're prepared to be honest with me, I'll be honest with you. Until then, accept that I know more about you than you'd ever guess—and I still want you."

If he read my journal, he wouldn't.

I jerk my chin out of his hand. Burns's eyes flash angrily. I expect him to grab me again, to prove that there's nothing of mine he won't take from me if he wants to, but he doesn't.

Instead, he rises up from the cot.

"You don't believe me."

I shrug. It's all I can do right now.

"Fine. I'll just have to prove that, too." Burns reaches into his pocket, pulling out a small, black box. "You're mine now, but you'll be mine forever. My lover. My angel." He pops the lid on it, revealing a shiny gold band. "My wife."

What?

Who walks around with a wedding band in their pocket? Who takes a woman hostage, propositions her for sex while she's cuffed and chained to a bed, then casually mentions that she'll be his wife one day? Who boasts about breaking into her apartment while she sleeps?

No one sane, of course.

This wasn't a crime of opportunity. He didn't see me, realize I was an easy target, and take me.

I gulp, refusing to acknowledge the wedding band he's holding. "How long were you planning this?"

Burns taps the crook of his elbow with the box. "Since the daisy, angel. Since the daisy."

THOUGH BURNS WAS PLEASED TO ADMIT THAT HE FOUND pleasure in watching me sleep, he leaves me alone in the basement after I tell him I'm tired and want to lie down. He refuses to until I eat the dinner he brings down for us to share, but once he's satisfied that I've had enough, he gives me my space.

I need it.

I'm a mess, something I don't want him to see. The whole day he was gone, I convinced myself that this was a mistake. That he could be reasoned with. That I could somehow make him let me go.

And then he showed me the wedding band and all my hopes of being back home by morning went up in smoke.

I can't sleep. I'm afraid of what will happen to me if I do, or what my subconscious will show me in the dark. I leave the light on, and doze fitfully. Never more than a few minutes at a time, though I don't have a clock down here with me so I have no freaking way of knowing how long it really is. I'm already up long before the sun starts streaming through the barred windows, though, and I feel like absolute shit when Burns comes down the next morning with breakfast.

The way his eyes rove over me, you'd think I was a supermodel, all decked out for a night on the town. In truth, I haven't showered in two days, my mouth tastes like ass, and my clothes are a disaster. My hair, too. I let it fall forward like a curtain, covering the deep purple bags under my eyes that have got to be there.

Since being his prisoner, I flip-flop from being defiant to withdrawn, then back again. No matter how many times Burns assures me that I'm safe with him, that he won't hurt me, I refuse to believe him. How can I?

When he sets the plate of scrambled eggs—my preference, though he didn't ask—in front of me, then a plastic spoon, I don't wait for him to tell me to eat. It's easy to just go along with it for now, and hope that he might slip up and bring me a utensil that I might be able to use against him.

I also would rather not let him feed me again. Like last night, I make sure to eat just enough to keep up my strength and prove to him that I'm not going on a hunger strike.

I do the same thing when he returns from his shift, bringing pizza with him. My mouth waters when I smell it, and my nervous stomach twitches with happiness when I see he got onions on half of it. Shocker: it's my favorite pizza topping. I also get the benefit of it doing something terrible to my breath, so though it's a pain in the ass to eat pizza with cuffed hands, I do.

My shoulders are aching. He purposely cuffed my hands on the outside of my sweater, the fabric forming a buffer between the metal and my skin, but the weight is still too much for my wrists.

Burns notices. While I eat, he climbs behind me on the cot, straddling my ass as he massages my neck, my back, and my shoulders. I went stiff when he first curved his big body around mine, then I went completely motionless as he wrapped his thick legs around me, pressing the bulge of his hard cock to the small of my back.

He doesn't do anything except knead my sore muscles with his hands. It's like they're fucking magical. At the moment, I forget that he's the reason I'm so uncomfortable, that if Burns hadn't cuffed me and left me like this for two days, I wouldn't need a massage. Taking another bite of pizza, I can't muffle the moan as I feel relaxed for the first time since I realized I was his captive.

That was my mistake. I let Burns think that, whatever he's doing, it's working. As I melted into him, he took advantage of it by brushing his lips along the side of my throat, peppering small kisses all the way up to my ear before taking the lobe between his teeth and biting just enough to have me gasping.

I should've pushed him away. I didn't. I just finish my pizza, then throw my head back, giving him easier access to my neck.

Taking heart in that, Burns grows bolder.

While one hand still rubs my shoulder, the other dips low. Reaching around me, he has the button on my jeans open before I realize exactly what he's doing.

All my tension returns. I go tight, even as he begins to tug on my zipper. "What... what are you doing?"

"I just want to pet you."

"Pet me?"

"Mmm." Another kiss to my throat. "I'll make you feel good if you let me."

I won't force you...

"What if I don't?"

My zipper is only tugged halfway down. Burns immediately releases it. "Then I'll stop. You're only delaying the inevitable, but if you don't want me to touch you tonight, I won't."

I swallow roughly.

He notices. His whisper sends shivers down my spine as he presses his mouth to my skin again. "What are you afraid of, angel?"

You.

Only... that's not true. I should be afraid of Burns. He's hot and cold. He goes from gentle to commanding in the blink of an eye. He'll take a kiss as his due, then try to cajole me into letting him into my pants. As if I could stop him if he really wanted to. He's got a head of height on me, a good fifty pounds, and obviously no morals.

He wants me. He took me. Why is this any different?

But it is. And I know, in this moment, that whatever happens next is going to set the stage for every other interaction we have while I'm his prisoner.

I'm right. I don't realize that until later, but I'm right.

And Burns proves that he knows me even better than he boasted last night because he offers me the one thing I can't refuse...

"Think of it as a trade."

"Trade?"

"Let me touch you and you can see how... accommodating I can be."

Accommodating?

Before I can ask what that means, he dips his fingers into his pocket. For a second, I wonder if he's going to show me the ring box again. He doesn't. He pulls out a tiny key instead. Then, fitting it into the minuscule hole on the cuffs, he pops the one on my right hand free.

Oh. I understand. I let him touch me, and he'll remove the cuff.

Only one, though, I discover as he leans back, murmuring in my ear, "Your hand for my fingers. What do you think, angel?"

I have to make sure. "Just your fingers?"

"For tonight, yes."

"Can I freshen up first?"

He chuckles. It's a low, husky laugh that bathes the back of my neck with his warm breath. "No need for that."

I disagree. "Burns, I—"

"Yes or no? Do I put the cuff back on, or will you let me play?"

When he puts it like that... "I guess yes, but—"

I don't even get to finish my sentence. The second I said 'yes', he already has his hand reaching past my jeans, past the band on my panties, burying his fingers in the curls covering my pussy. I jump, but Burns's hand on my shoulder holds me down. As he starts to explore, fingers brushing past my clit, searching for my entrance, sliding through my slick pussy folds, he keeps me right where he wants me.

"Oh, angel. I don't know why you tried to deny the both of us. I thought I would have to work to get you wet but... *fuck me*... you're *soaked*."

I am. I refuse to think about why, but considering I can hear his fingers moving, I can't deny it.

"You won't last long like this," he announces to my sudden shame. He should have to work for it, but I'm already starting to pant a little as he slips one of his big fingers about an inch inside of me. "My good girl... you're so fucking tight. You haven't let another man touch you like this in a while, huh? It's like you knew you needed me."

I want to splash a cold dose of reality on Burns. It might not put out the fire completely, but maybe it'll help. "I'm not a virgin, you know."

"What the fuck would I want with a virgin?" he retorts, shocking me. "Sex for the first time is awkward. It's not fun. We both got that shit out of the way. All I care about is that there's no one else for either of us now. So what if I wasn't the first? Being the last is all I give a shit about. And that starts tonight."

The whole time he was talking, he was working his finger inside of me as far as he can go with this angle. Considering how stretched I feel now, it's not just one. Two, at least, and as though he's mimicking fucking me with his dick, he's stroking in and out.

Just like that, Burns has claimed me with his fingers—and I was too distracted by his husky voice to notice.

Not anymore.

"*Oh*."

It's a soft whimper, more for the feeling of his fingers than how determined he sounded when he told me there wouldn't be anyone else for me after him, but I make it.

And he hears it.

"Oh?" he echoes. "Is that all you have to say?"

I nod.

From behind me, he huffs. "Then I'm not doing a good enough job of petting you, am I?"

EIGHT
GIVE IN

ANGELA

I'm not prepared for how quickly my captor moves.

One second, I'm basically on his lap. The next? He removes his fingers, climbs out from behind me, and leaves the cot. I'm only missing his touch for a few seconds before he grips my shoulder with one hand, easing me to my back.

Taking one of my hands, he presses a close-mouthed kiss to the middle of my palm.

While I marvel over the gentle gesture so at odds with the bruising hold on my shoulder, as though he's adamant that I can't escape him even in this intimacy, he turns on me again, grabbing my jeans with a fierceness that has me gasping as he yanks them down past my ass.

He leaves them around my thighs, trapping me almost completely as his cuffs do. I couldn't even kick my legs at him if I thought it would help, and I'm merciless to his whims as he snatches the fabric of my admittedly damp panties next.

Another tug, another gasp. The fabric gets lost in my jeans as he bares my pussy completely to the hunger in his gaze.

"Ah." He grins. It's a predator's smile, the grin of a man who likes what he sees—and who knows with absolute certainty that he owns it. "That's better."

Keeping his eyes on my face, watching my expression, Burns returns his fingers to my heat, that shark-like grin widening when I moan this time at how full I feel before clutching his arm with my free hand when he increases how fast he's pumping into me.

"That's my angel," he rumbles, flicking my engorged clit with his thumb as he develops a rhythm. "Take my fingers like a good girl. I want those moans. I've *earned* them. And when you come on my hand, just think about how much better it'll be when I get my cock inside of you."

He says it like it's an inevitability. And, heaven help me, but as I throw my head back, letting him do whatever he wants to me, I almost want to beg for him to replace his fingers with his dick.

But I can't. I already let him take too much. These sensations are *too much*. This was only supposed to be a simple petting, a way for Burns to get what he wanted while I didn't have to sacrifice more than I was willing to to win some freedom back.

And now? His expert touch on my achy body has turned into a race for a climax that I... I don't really know that I'm ready for.

Come on my hands... that's exactly what he's demanding of me. And, as though he knows exactly how close I am to doing just that, Burns starts to bark orders at me.

That's the cop in him, I guess—or the controlling, demanding lover that I'm willing to bet he is no matter who he has in his bed.

"That's it. You're doing so fucking beautifully. Now lift your ass."

When I'm too slow to obey, he tweaks my clit. It's not a pinch, not quite, but it sends tremors down my already shaky legs.

I don't know if it's a grunt or a squeal I let out at the fresh wave of sensation and *need* that rushes through me, but whatever it is, Burns wants more.

"I said lift your ass, angel. Even if it's just my fingers, I'm gonna fuck you as deep as I can."

There's a threat in his deep voice. If I refuse him, he might forget himself and reach for his own zipper.

It's hard, with Burns's big body right there and one

hand still cuffed to the headboard. I'm breathing heavy, trying to fight the orgasm about to hit, but I do just what he ordered. I lift my ass, shifting my hip toward him, nearly howling when his fingers enter me at a different angle and my whole body tightens.

"Yes," he purrs. "I knew you would react just like this. Like you were made for me. Like your body *knows* mine. Because I know yours, angel. And I know you're just fucking dying to come. So do it. Give it to me."

Give it to me...

If I do, it's giving in to the twisted cop who thought he could just take me and I'd do whatever he says.

And, damn it, haven't I given him enough already?

I let him touch me even when I knew I shouldn't. I gave him permission to stroke me, even spread out for him here willingly while he dipped his fingers inside of me, owning me from the inside out.

But if I do this... if I climax while he works my body like this... it's letting him win.

Defiant Angela has finally decided to make an appearance. To deny her captor what he wants, she'll deny herself *everything*.

"You can do it." His voice has almost turned pleading. He wants me to find release with him. It's not just ownership now, it's a gift he's demanding... and I just can't bring myself to do it, even as his tone turns cajoling. "Let yourself go."

Uh-uh.

No.

I shake my head, stubbornly clinging to this one thing. He needs to know that I'm not going to be his pet. I'm not going to be his willing prisoner.

He took me. He thinks he knows me.

No one really does—and it's time Officer Burns finds that out.

So I shake my head, even though it probably seems more like I'm thrashing on the cot.With the cuff tethering me to the headboard, and Burns's hand pinning me in place while the other plays with my clit like it's his favorite toy, it's impossible to actually get away from him.

He knows it, too. He knows I'm at his mercy.

I have been since the daisy.

I don't care. It's a battle of wills at this point, and I need this if I'm ever going to hold my own against Burns. Because, if I show him how good it feels to have him touching me, it'll only let him think that he was right to take me.

To make me his prisoner.

I *won't*—

—at least, not until Burns gets a determined look on his handsome face as he bows over me. Before I know what he's thinking, he squeezes one of my boobs, finding my nipple through the padding on my bra.

It's a different sensation, one I wasn't prepared for. As I try to escape his hand on my tit, he pulls his slick fingers out of my pussy, jams them back in, and uses his thumb to rub frantically the top of my clit once he's fully seated inside of me.

As soon as he does that, the choice is no longer mine.

I let out a keening cry that has Burns's dark blue eyes lighting up.

This man is an enigma to me, but I can read his expression easily. It's part victory, part pleasure, as though he got off just knowing he stole my orgasm like a damn trophy.

The same way he stole *me*.

And there's that grin again.

"No one has to know," he tells me, a split second before he covers my body with his. Gripping my chin with the hand covered with my slickness, he takes my mouth in a punishing kiss that swallows my cry, taking it inside of him.

He squeezes when I don't respond to how dominatingly his tongue plunders its way into my mouth. Only when I kiss him back as much as I can with his hand a burning brand against my lower jaw, does he release me.

He's triumphant as he licks his bottom lip. Then, his gaze locked on mine, he slips his fingers into his mouth. He laves them clean, then tucks them under my chin, forcing me to keep my eyes on him.

"Don't regret it, angel. And don't feel bad that I made you come the hardest you ever had before. It's okay. This can be our secret."

This time, when he kisses me, he nips my bottom lip with his teeth. It doesn't hurt, but it's just another way for Burns to prove to me that he owns me.

He doesn't pull away. Instead, lips brushing against mine, so close I feel the heat of his breath, he whispers, "Just like you were made to be my dirty little secret."

And that's when I realize that there's something really wrong with me.

I never wanted to give him my release, but the orgasm that began when he grabbed my boob and jabbed his thumb into my clit suddenly becomes a second full-blown, leg-shaking climax as he pins me down on the cot with his uniformed body, stealing a kiss while promising—in his own way—that what passed between us belongs *only* to us.

Because, whether I like it or not, until Burns lets me go, there *is* an us.

I can't help it. Needing something to cling to as I ride out the second orgasm, I wrap my free arm around as much of him as I can as I fall apart into the cot, moaning into his smirk.

Only when I'm panting softly, coming down from the high, does he finally ease his weight off of me. As though it's only right, Burns joins me on the cot, lying on his side so that his brawny, muscular body can squeeze on the small mattress next to my exhausted one.

I'm still panting. Whether it's from an overload of pleasure or simple frustration that he played my damn body like a violin, I can't tell. I'm not sure I want to. Swallowing the lump lodged in my throat, my eyelashes flutter, my gaze a little unfocused as I stare up at the ceiling over our heads.

Burns doesn't like that. I should've known better.

He needs my eyes on him.

So, with the same sticky fingers from before, he takes my chin in his hand. It's a much gentler grip that he uses to guide me toward him.

And there he is.

Dark.

Commanding.

Beautiful, yet terrifying.

And, for as long as he wants to keep me, *mine*— whether I want him to be or not.

I've honestly never seen such a self-satisfied grin on any guy's face as they gazed down at me until now. More than anything, it's so damn proud.

So undeniably *male,* and I'm the woman who put that look there.

Even worse? If he decided to push me right now, I

don't know if I'd refuse him again. Because knowing that I pleased him by letting him fingerfuck me?

Something must really be wrong with me, because I *like* it.

"No one has to know," he echoes softly around that daring grin.

Yeah.

Except I already do.

———

I SLEPT WITH ONE HAND CUFFED TO THE HEADBOARD. THE other was cuffed to Burns who refused to leave me alone after he made me come.

All night, his big body bracketed mine, spread out on the small cot to the point that I either hung off the side or laid beside him, the heat from his hip and his thigh warming me up a whole lot more than the blanket he pulled over us before commanding me to go to sleep.

I did. Whether it was the endorphins that did it or last night's restlessness, I slept dreamlessly through the night.

What else could I do?

Trying to break free from the headboard was one thing. With Burns smart enough to cuff my right hand to his left before joining me on the mattress, I gave up any hope of escaping. I hadn't slept in the two nights since I woke up from the drugs he pumped into me, and after the way he refused to stop until he had wrung another orgasm out of me, I was mentally, physically, and emotionally exhausted. While falling asleep next to my captor seems reckless, I couldn't help myself. Almost as though his touch was as much a sedative as a drug, my sleep wasn't just dreamless. It was unbroken until I woke up to the sound of someone clearing their throat.

My arm aches. It's still stretched over my head, the metal cuff clanging against the headboard as I try to stretch it out. There's enough give that I can bend my elbow, trying to work the kink out of my arm.

As much as that aches, it's nothing compared to how tender my pussy feels. To my surprise, my captor was insistent in his pursuit of making me come, yet not as rough as I would've expected from someone who wanted to take, take, *take*. Still, just like he said to me, it has been years since anyone's touched me like he did. Whether it was his dick or his fingers, it didn't matter. He penetrated me, and now that I'm not on the verge of coming again, I'm feeling it this morning.

I hear a chuckle. I'd completely forgotten that I wasn't alone, though I'm the only one in the small bed right now. At that realization, my eyes spring open. There, standing a few feet away from the cot, is Burns.

He's in his uniform again. His dark hair is freshly

washed and styled, his gun in its holster, his handcuffs hanging off his hip.

I can still feel one pair biting into my skin, keeping me cuffed to the bed. But if he's there, and he has another, what about...

My left hand is completely free this time. Instead of making it so that both of my hands are cuffed together like they have been, or chaining me to another part of the cot, he's actually allowed me full use of one of my hands at least.

I glance over at him. Burns smirks.

"I keep my promises, angel. My fingers for your hand, like I said. See? I can be accommodating, too."

Good for him. I shake the hand attached to the headboard, jangling the cuff. "What about this one?"

"Oh? You want both of them free?" Dipping his hand into the pocket of his uniform pants, Burns pulls out the same key he used on me last night. He twirls it between his forefinger and his thumb. "Tell me... what would you do for this? For your freedom?"

Honestly? A lot more than I would ever want to confess to my captor. To have my hands free, I'd go even farther than I did last night, no matter how ashamed I am to admit that.

Not like I do. Because, instead of telling him what I would be willing to do to get my hand free, I turn the question around on him.

"Depends. What do you want from me?"

"You already know what I want, angel. But since you're not ready to accept that, let's start at the beginning. Kiss me."

That's all?

It's just further proof that he doesn't know me at all. If he had an idea what he could get away with, he wouldn't make this so easy right now.

In fact, since he doesn't know... maybe it's time I see what *I* can get away with.

NINE
DEAL WITH THE DEVIL

ANGELA

I bite down on my bottom lip. "What if I don't want to?"

"I'd say that you already did last night, angel. What's one more?"

"You kissed me last night," I remind him.

"You're absolutely right. And that's precisely why I think you should kiss me if you want this key." He twirls it again, drawing my attention to the small piece of metal. "Are you desperate enough to give me what I want? Or would you rather spend my whole shift cuffed to the cot until I come home to you?"

I think it over.

As much as it sucked to have my hands cuffed together, at least I could get up and use the toilet and the sink. I was able to walk around, too, pacing the basement while trying to figure out my next move.

No way I can do that if I'm handcuffed to the head-board for the whole day. I'll be stuck in one spot, forced to either hold my pee in or piss the mattress if I can't, and that's only one downside I can think of being trapped to the cot.

So he gave me one hand back, just like he said he would. It won't do me any good if I'm stuck here, will it? Not unless I can get him to take off the other cuff—and, to do that, I have to give in to him.

Again.

Burns really is a tricky bastard. I'll have to remember that...

He runs his free hand through his dark hair, then scratches the edge of his jaw idly as he continues to smile down at me.

I know right away to brace myself for what's coming next.

"You want your freedom, Angela? I want my forever. And I'm the one in charge here. But I'm feeling generous. Can't say it'll last, so I'd take the chance while you can. Kiss me, and I'll take off the cuffs for good."

My heart starts racing as I try to realize where I can lose this time. Because, one thing for sure, he's playing for keeps. I'm playing for something else.

Maybe it's time I make a move.

I hold up a finger. "Just... one kiss?"

"To start. Do we have a deal?"

A deal with the devil, maybe, but if there's one thing I learned from last night, it's that he stands by his word if he gives it.

"Yes."

He crouches down so he's in front of me. "See. I'm not so bad," he breathes out. "Your freedom for one measly kiss."

Only it won't be. Not my freedom, or just one kiss.

I know *that* much for sure.

Burns has made it clear since I woke up in this basement that, until he's done with me one way or another, I'm not going anywhere. His endgame is... actually, I have no idea *what* it is. If I can believe him, it's a shotgun wedding.

At the very least, there's no way he won't be satisfied until I let him fuck me. For now, though, he wants a kiss.

As intimate as it was to let him draw off my panties and finger me, initiating a kiss on my own seems even more so.

"Uncuff me first."

I didn't think he'd rise to my dare, but he does.

Without even a moment's hesitation, he rises up and moves over to the headboard, using his key to release the cuff from it. I notice that he doesn't remove the one from my wrist. Probably because he wants to make sure I do give him the kiss I promised him before he does.

Fair enough. I can play this little game with him as well as he can.

Burns wants a kiss? I'll give him one.

With my hands free at all, I push myself up from the cot. Once I'm standing—because laying on the mattress with Burns is bad, bad idea—I gesture for him to come closer to me.

He moves into me. Once he's within my reach, he ducks his dark head, so trustingly that I have to wonder what game he's playing now.

I'm free. He allowed it himself. I could swing the metal handcuff across his face at this distance, stunning him long enough to... I don't know... grab his gun or something.

But I don't, and even I can't quite understand why. Instead, proving to him that I can be a good girl when I choose to be, I go up on my tippy-toes and rest my palms against his hard jaw.

His stubble pricks the inside of my hand. The look on his face sense a shiver down my spine.

Waiting for me to actually do this, he defiantly keeps his mouth closed. He's not going to make this easy for me. To even initiate the kiss, he forces me to press my lips against his first , licking at the seam of his mouth, begging for entrance.

I'm beginning to understand my captor. He'll

accept nothing less than a kiss that I've controlled completely from the start, and maybe it's the stubborn side of me peeking through, but I absolutely refuse to give up until he lets me inside of him this time.

He manipulated me into doing this. Even as Burns opens his mouth, immediately taking the kiss over once our tongues touch, I'm aware of it.

That doesn't stop me from continuing to respond to every move he makes, does it?

After he's gone again, leaving me alone in my basement cell, I rub my fingertip over my lips, savoring his taste.

So maybe I let the insane cop who kidnapped me fingerfuck me to orgasm, then blackmail me into kissing him on my own accord.

On the plus side, my hands are finally free—and, so far, he hasn't tried to slip that ring he keeps in that box in his pocket on my finger yet.

And isn't that something to be grateful for?

ANOTHER DAY ALONE IN THE BASEMENT. ANOTHER DAY OF waiting for Burns to return from his patrol.

He never removed the cuff. My hands are free, but the heavy weight of the one cuff is a constant reminder that I'm still as much his prisoner as I was when I first woke up down here.

I ate. I read the first three chapters of my botany guide before my mind began to wander. When my thoughts kept returning to my captor instead of the flowers I was reading about, I slammed the cover shut before returning to the cot.

I tried to nap. It didn't work.

What I wouldn't give for my phone. Not because I thought it would do anything after the way Burns always sent messages to the few people I actually was in contact with, but because it has games. I had streaming apps. Mindless videos would make my time alone go by so much faster.

I asked Burns about it last night before he scooted me to the side of the cot, squeezing his big body in next to me right after he cuffed us together; even in sleep, he wanted to make sure I couldn't get away from him. All he said was that, if I was good, I would get rewarded.

Too bad that's easier said than done...

Finally, when it feels like I've been waiting forever, the door to the basement creaks open.

I sit up, watching warily as Burns slowly descends into the basement. What kind of captor will I get today, I wonder? Fierce? Playful? Commanding? Possessive?

Horny?

From what I've learned about Burns, it's probably a combination of all five—but mostly horny.

He's not the only one. And I'm not sure what that says about me that I can be attracted to the dark cop who took me prisoner, but maybe if Mason Burns wasn't as gorgeous as he was, I might stand a chance.

Coming home from work, I see that he didn't change out of his uniform. Not completely, at least. As though he started to, then got distracted, his uniform shirt is open, his sculpted chest on display. It's the first glimpse I've gotten of the man beneath the badge and... yeah.

I can't help but stare. And why shouldn't I? Everything I've learned about him since I woke up his personal prisoner says that he's been stalking me, watching me, sneaking into my apartment while I was vulnerable and unaware... who knows what else he's done? If I can get a little of my own back by objectifying him, I'm going to.

It would be so much easier if he was a troll. If he was unattractive, his outsides matching just how broken he is on the inside. But he's not. He's too handsome for his own good; worse, he knows it. He wields his deceptively charming smile as more of a weapon as his gun, and silly me, I fell for it.

So distracted by the peek of his chest he's giving me, I didn't notice that he's carrying something with him until he lays it down on the cot, next to where I'm sitting on the edge. It's a dry-cleaning bag attached to a hanger. I have no idea what could be inside of it, and

I don't get the chance to ask before Burns is looming right in front of me.

"Miss me, angel?"

"No."

Crouching low, he grips my chin with his fingers. He uses just enough pressure so that it's a pinch, but he doesn't hurt me. He tilts my head back, a crooked smile on his lips. "You're a fucking liar." His tongue darts out, swiping over the height of my cheek. "But that means you missed me so I'll let it pass. Especially because I missed you."

Another pinch and my lips part. Burns takes advantage, swooping in and taking another claiming kiss. I haven't brushed my teeth in days. It can't taste good, but you wouldn't know from the satisfied smirk tugging on his lips as he pulls back enough to look right into my eyes.

"I expect a kiss 'hello' whenever I finish a shift." He lets go of my chin, though he doesn't put any distance between us. In fact, he inches forward so that all I see, all I scent, all I *know* is Mason Burns. "Now be a good girl and kiss your cop."

"But you... I just did."

His eyes sparkle in amusement. Of course. If there's one thing I learned so far, it's that when he gets what he wants, Burns is in a good mood. When he doesn't... I haven't forgotten the way he lost his temper and shot the bullet-resistant cinder block walls.

"No. I kissed you. Now you kiss me."

I don't argue. If he thinks there's a difference, fine. Besides, what was it he said to me this morning? One measly kiss?

I knew he would never stop at one. But if this is all he demands from me, I guess it could be worse. Especially since it isn't long before Burns takes control over the second kiss. Still, I must've done something right because, as soon as he breaks the kiss, he finally releases me from the last cuff.

I immediately rub my wrist. It feels so good not to be wearing them anymore.

"Is this because I kissed you?" I have to know where we are in this little tit for tat we have going.

"No."

Oh. "Then... why?"

He smirks, but doesn't answer me. Instead, he grabs the dry-cleaning bag. "I have something for you."

Unzipping it, he shakes off the covering, revealing—

"A dress?" I ask.

That's what it is. A skimpy-looking red cocktail dress.

Burns nods. "I had to watch you go on a date with

another man. It's only fair that you make it up to me by being mine tonight."

Mine...

"What... what do you mean by that?"

"It's simple. We're going to have dinner together. A real meal. I've got candles. Restaurant take-out from that Italian place by your apartment. Obviously, we can't go out, but, make no mistake, you're my date tonight."

When I went out with Dean, I wore a simple sweater and my best pair of jeans. That's nothing like the dress that Burns brought me. Other than that, my captor is recreating the last date I had before he "arrested" me. He even went to the trouble of ordering from Mamma Maria's, and I bet you everything I have —which isn't much—that, somehow, he got me the same meal I always eat when I splurge on a dinner there.

If so, it's just another reminder that he *does* know me. And I... I don't know what to make of that at all.

Swallowing the sudden lump lodged in my throat, I just say, "I'm not hungry for a big meal."

"Then we'll just have to work up an appetite." He pauses for dramatic effect, the bastard. "In the shower."

Good thing that lump is gone because I choke. "What?"

"Have you taken one?"

"No. I... with the cuffs—"

There's not even a lick of shame as he says, "Yes. With your hands cuffed, it would've been a bitch to take a shower. Hands are free now, though, aren't they? I thought you'd like to freshen up for our date. Of course, to make sure you don't try anything while you're in there, I'll have to join you. Once you're done" —he lifts up the dress again—"you can wear this for me."

I'll wear the dress. Honestly, I'll wear anything if I can get out of the clothes I've been stuck in for days.

But the shower?

"I... I'm not taking a shower with you, Burns."

"Is that so?"

I nod.

If he forces me to, I won't be able to refuse. We both know that. If he tries to convince me the same way he got me to agree to let him finger me, he'll win. I still can't quite figure out how that happened. Burns is too persuasive for my own good, I guess, and as much as I'd love a shower right now, it wouldn't take much for him to push me into saying 'yes'.

To my surprise, he doesn't. Oh, he manipulates me. I'm beginning to think that's the MO with this cop. I walked right into his trap by immediately refusing him, and I realize that as soon as he says, "Fine. But if I give you privacy in the shower, you'll have to give me something, too."

I'm afraid to find out what he has in mind. "Like what?"

"I won't join you, but I will watch you."

"Shower?"

"Undress."

Yup. He caught me—or, rather, he thinks he did.

Know what? I've been wearing the same clothes for days. He bunched my sweater high, shimmying down my pants, baring my pussy to him last night. With the tattoo on my tit, I know he's seen at least one. Put that all together, and I've basically been naked in front of him before.

Even better, if I agree, I get the upper hand. Does Burns see it like that? Probably not. I do. It makes sense in my head.

I'll own my nudity so that he can't.

"Okay."

He raises his eyebrows. "Yeah?"

"Yeah."

"Go on. I'm ready when you are."

Folding his hands behind his head, Burns sprawls out on the cot. I have to climb over him to get off of it, and when he runs his finger over my ass as I do, I pretend not to notice.

Before I think better of what I'm doing, I start to take off my clothes. I don't go for seductive. This isn't some kind of striptease for my obsessed stalker. This is me, showing him what he can't have while doing just enough to keep the scales balanced between us.

It doesn't matter what my intentions are. As soon as I'm completely naked, Burns thumbs the corner of his mouth, eyes gone dark with lust as he takes me in.

"Forget the dress, angel," he says, his voice gone hoarse. "This is all I want to see you in tonight."

Yeah... not if I can help it.

TEN
JUST HIS TONGUE

ANGELA

When I'm finally done with my shower, there's a towel waiting for me on the top of the toilet, plus a tube of A&D ointment.

I guess Burns left these for me while I was behind the frosted glass door of the standing shower. After his confession that he used to break into my apartment to watch me sleep, I wouldn't put it past him to stand there and stare as I showered. So consumed with washing my captivity off of me, I don't think I would've cared even if he did.

He really was prepared for me. He had my favored brand of shampoo and conditioner waiting inside the stall, a vanilla-scented body wash, and some antibacterial soap. That, like the ointment, is a big clue that he wants me to take care of the tattoo he left on my chest.

I almost refused. I feel like it'll only work against me if I do everything that Burns expects me to without putting up even a little fight. However, trapped in this basement cell, what exactly will happen if I develop an infection because I was too stubborn to take care of his mark? If I get out of this in one piece, I can always get his name and number removed. I can't do that if I die of sepsis.

I don't have any tattoos. I've always thought about getting one, though, so I've done my research. In the shower, I peeled the bandage off, letting it breathe while I scrubbed the rest of my body and washed my hair. Using the antibacterial soap, I washed the tattoo. Patting it dry with the towel, I applied the ointment.

There. It's as good as it's going to get. Here's hoping I didn't screw up somehow.

Glancing around, I can't find a brush. Not a hair-brush, at least. There's a brand new toothbrush next to the sink and—no surprise—the brand of toothpaste I use at home. Taking the hint for what it is, I brush my teeth, then finger comb my hair.

At that point, I realize that, if I stay in the bath-room much longer, Burns is going to get impatient and come in so he can drag me back out.

Hoping like hell that Burns won't really make me parade around naked in front of him, I tighten my grip on the towel. It doesn't cover much. My cleavage is on display—so is the shiny tattoo—and the hem of the towel barely hits the curve of my ass.

He's been busy while I was in the shower. The small table has two candles, each with a flickering flame casting shadows in the corner of the basement. Two plates are set, facing each other. Just like I thought, one of them has a plate of ravioli on it; that one has to be mine. The other has eggplant parmigiana, I think. I can't really tell, only that Burns is gonna have a hard time eating it if he insists on only bringing plastic spoons around me.

As though I didn't already spend a good chunk of this afternoon trying to figure out how to make a sturdy shiv out of a plastic spoon...

Hey. I watch a lot of prison shows. It might not have prepared me for living with an insane cop, but if it helps me figure out a way to escape, it would've been well worth it.

It smells delicious. I don't even pretend like I'm not going to eat dinner now. Looks like Burns was right. I definitely worked up an appetite in the shower.

He's waiting for me just outside of the bathroom. In his hand, he's traded the dress from before for a light grey t-shirt that he hands to me with a smirking, "For you."

I shake it out. A familiar logo stares back at me. It's an SPD shirt. Springfield Police Department.

I know what it is. I'm just not so sure why he's giving it to me. "What's this?"

"One of my shirts. I thought you could wear it while we eat."

"What about the dress?" Considering Burns is both taller and larger than me, if I wear a shirt that's his size, it might actually cover more of me than that skimpy red dress. Definitely more than the towel I currently have on.

"Next time, angel. Tonight, I want you in something of mine. Unless you'd rather go naked? Because I won't mind."

I quickly shrug the t-shirt on over my head. It musses my damp hair. Shoving it out of my face, I ask, "No underwear?"

The look he gives me answers the question. Right. No underwear.

Because the table is so low to the ground, we sit on the floor to eat. I yelp when the t-shirt shifts and my bare ass hits the cool cement. For some reason, Burns finds that amusing. He does get up, grabbing the blanket from the cot, laying it beneath me so that I have some coverage, so I guess I can forgive him for his slight smirk at my expense.

Dinner tastes as delicious as it smells. Usually, I don't like reheating my food in the microwave, but Mamma Maria's is an hour away from where I currently am. Between cold food and a nuked meal,

I'm glad Burns thought to warm it up. And watching him struggle to cut the eggplant parm with the plastic spoon is as funny to me as I thought.

He's a smart man, though. After so many years of sleeping with a knife under my pillow for protection, I'm more comfortable than I probably should be with the idea of stabbing him if it'll get me my freedom. Pity each one of my homemade shivs has snapped with too much pressure, but if there's one thing I have right now, it's plenty of freaking time to figure it out.

I finish first; scooping up the ravioli with the spoon is a lot easier, I admit. As I watch Burns eat, his gaze grows more and more heavy-lidded as he stares back at me. I don't know what kind of thoughts are running through his head. Considering he's basically fucking me with his eyes, I'm betting he's seeing right through his old t-shirt, imagining me naked again.

It's something like that all right...

As soon as he finishes eating, he looks right at me and announces, "I'm ready for dessert."

Mamma Mia has an extensive dessert menu. For a moment, I honestly believe that's what he means. There's a black box resting on top of the fridge that I think he's referring to, so when he gets up, I figure he's going for that.

I'm wrong. Burns is coming right at me.

Standing behind me, he hooks his hands under my arms. Next thing I know, I'm on my feet—but that doesn't last. He swings me up in his arms, carrying me bridal-style across the basement before laying me out on the bed.

Still too naive to understand just what his plans are, I don't get his 'dessert' quip until he moves to the foot of the cot, frame squeaking under his weight as he climbs up. Then, with one of my ankles in each of his big hands, he opens my legs to him. The SPD shirt rode up enough that I'm completely naked from the waist down.

Burns wedges his shoulders in the gap he created, eyes locked on the juncture between my legs.

And I finally understand what he meant.

I try to slam my legs shut. Absolutely impossible with a brawny cop in the way.

He dips his head, leaving no question about what exactly he plans on eating for dessert.

Me.

"Burns," I squeal. "What are you doing?"

"Isn't it obvious?" With my legs spread, his mouth inches from my pussy, he looks up at me. "I got a taste of you last night. I licked every damn drop from my fingers, but I was a fucking fool if I thought that would be enough. I've thought about doing this the entire time I was on patrol. Are you telling me that you don't want this?"

I do. Damn it. I wish it wasn't true, but considering he's got a front row seat to my pussy, he can tell that

I'm already beginning to get ready for him. No denying that the idea of any guy licking me to orgasm doesn't turn me on, but there's something so... so *heady* about it being Burns wanting to do it.

But I know better now. Tit for tat, right?

"Wait. Okay? I gotta know first... if you do this for me, what do I have to do for you?"

"Oh, angel... you've got it wrong. You let me fuck you with my tongue and I'll owe you."

I... he's joking, right? I've been with a couple of guys who would insist on head, then shove their dicks inside of me, bounce a couple of times, then blow their load. If I even mentioned the idea they might want to reciprocate, they acted like the idea of putting their mouth willingly somewhere they had no problem sticking their dick into was a problem.

I got lucky once or twice. A few of my boyfriends were willing to give me a couple of licks here or there. Even they made it seem like they were doing me a favor.

And Burns is—in his stilted way—almost pleading with me to let him do this?

"Just your tongue?" I ask.

"I promise."

I admit, this is one slippery slope. I know that.

Just your fingers...

Just one kiss...

Just your tongue.

Sooner or later, it's going to be *just the tip,* then *as long as you don't come in me...* but, right now, I don't care. While he waits for my answer, Burns blew a gentle gust of air right on top of my mound. If he doesn't start licking, I might grab his head and shove it right against my pussy.

"Fine. But just your tongue."

No need for that. The second I give him my condition, he grips me beneath my hip, slides me toward him, and buries his nose against me.

Like last night, he doesn't take it easy. As though he knows exactly how much I can handle, he goes right for what he wants. Between sucking my folds into his mouth, licking the entire length of my slit, and nuzzling my clit, he feasts on my pussy as though I hadn't just watched him eat an entire meal.

I squeal again the first time he dips his tongue inside of me, fucking me that way like he said he would. When he adds his fingers to the mix, opening me wide so he can lap up every bit of wetness I give him, I go almost cross-eyed with pleasure.

At some point I do give up and close my eyes. I ride out two separate orgasms on his tongue, and when I whimper that I can't take another one, Burns conveniently doesn't understand what I'm saying as I pant out my pleas for him to take it easy on me. Why I thought to expect mercy from Mason Burns, I don't know, and by the time he rips a third orgasm out of me, I'm ready to pass out completely.

Luckily, he finally leaves me alone after I threaten to kick him in the face if he doesn't. I'm bluffing, of course. With that much pleasure wrung from me, I doubt I could lift my leg at all. It works, though, and as much as I miss his touch, it's for the best.

I almost fall asleep then and there. The only reason I don't is because I sense his return and I'm not so sure I can believe that he really doesn't expect me to reciprocate.

I got off three times. Even more, if you count last night. How much longer until he expects me to do something for him?

"Open wide, Angela."

My eyes spring open. For a split second, I expect to see his dick in my face.

It's not. He has a spoon in his hand, lifted in front of my face. He waits until I do open my mouth, then tilts it inside. "Here's your dessert."

It's... cake. Red velvet, my favorite.

Shocker.

As I chew, I can't quite hide how tasty it is.

He notices. Feeding me another bite, as though he's taking pleasure out of seeing me enjoy it, he smirks. "Told you, angel. Good girls get rewarded."

ELEVEN
A TRAP

ANGELA

The cake isn't the only thing Burns gives me that night.

Though he insists on me sleeping in his cop shirt, he reveals that he made a pit stop at my apartment, packing me a bag full of my own clothes. Not much. He has to know my focus is getting him to lower his guard so I can escape him, but like getting him to remove the cuffs and having the chance to shower, he rewards me with something other to wear than a cocktail dress and the same outfit I've slept in for days.

I'm not allowed to change out of his SPD shirt. That's fine. It's actually pretty comfy.

However, in an act of total defiance, I grab one of the pairs of panties he actually shoved in the bag and pull them on right in front of him.

He laughs. Of course he does. "If you think that'll keep me from my pussy, go right ahead, angel. But don't be mad when I rip them off of you."

Understandably, I'm not so keen on falling asleep next to him after that comment. I don't have any choice about that, either. Burns doesn't chain us together, but with the weight of his leg thrown over mine, his arm wrapping around me, I'm as good as tethered to him. I don't move. It doesn't matter. He's hard from the moment he curves his big body by mine, though the only mention he makes of sex is his crack about my panties.

I still find it hard to knock out. The bliss following my orgasm has turned to confusion. I hate how easy it is for Burns to convince me to let him do whatever he wants to my body. Every time I decide to stand firm, to treat him like a deranged captor, he turns on that charming smile and that filthy, possessive mouth and I... I give in.

I wish I could explain it. I think it's a new type of trauma response for me. After seeing how my life was ruined because I didn't go along with giving Carter everything he wanted, I'm quick to offer it to Burns if only because he's made sex so transactional.

I'm not letting him touch me because I want *him*.

It's what I can get out of him that makes me so fucking agreeable.

And I want freedom.

On my fourth day of captivity, I get a tiny slice of it.

Pity it doesn't last.

In the four days that I've been trapped in Burns's basement, I've developed a bit of a routine. He's gone for the bulk of the daylight hours, so there's plenty of time to kill. When my attention span allows it, I lose myself in my book about flowers. It's the one thing saving my sanity, I think.

In another life, I would've been a botanist. In the quiet of this underground space, I convince myself I still can.

I pace a lot. Sleep, too. When the four walls seem like they're closing in on me, I climb the steps and rattle the doorknob. It's always locked, but I'd never forgive myself if I didn't check.

The same thing happens on the fourth day.

After breakfast and another demanded kiss, Burns heads out in his uniform. Like I have been, I wait until enough minutes have passed that, even if he left the door open, I won't run into him on his way to his cop car. Today, that's about ten minutes.

Tiptoeing up the stairs, I grab the handle, fully expecting it to be locked.

It isn't.

I don't stop to think. I don't stop to wonder if it's a coincidence, or if it's a trap.

It's a trap.

Flinging the door open, I find myself in a homy-looking living room. I don't see Burns, though my quick looks reveals a big screen TV, an unlit fireplace, a leather couch, and two pairs of shoes set side by side.

One is obviously a pair of Burns's uniform shoes. The other? The boots I was wearing on my date with Dean.

A bubble of insane laughter wells up inside of me. The whole time I've been trapped in Burns's base-ment, barefoot, I wondered what happened to my boots. All along, he's had them set up right next to his, like they belong there.

Like *I* belong here.

You've gotta be kidding me.

Don't care. Right now, I just don't care. Those are my shoes, and I only stop long enough to shove my feet inside of them so I can bolt for the front door.

The second I get outside, the first thing I notice is that it's pouring. Like, skies opened up, water sluicing down-type of rain. I'm almost blinded by it, the force of the rain nearly flattening me as I take my first steps toward freedom.

They're short-lived. Almost immediately, one hand goes to my throat, the other my waist, and I'm being lifted from the dirt and dragged away from the doorway.

My head swivels. Drenched from head to toe, his hair impossibly black thanks to the rain, I find Burns holding me.

"Burns? What are you doing here?"

"Weren't expecting me?"

No. He was supposed to be on his way to work, and I was supposed to be on my way to freedom.

"I—"

"I'm off duty. Don't go back to Springfield for two days."

It hits me. The door wasn't unlocked by accident. He left it that way. Just like how he waited just out of sight, standing in the pouring rain, waiting to see what I would do if I discovered the door was unlocked.

He's absolutely bonkers. Dangerous, too. And tricky.

Worse, I can't believe I forgot that for even a second.

Struggling against his hold, I gasp. "You tricked me?"

He moves us under the slim awning on the roof of the cabin I just escaped. Lowering me to my feet, he cages my body with one arm. The other? His hand goes right to my throat.

So do his lips.

Crazy fucker starts kissing my throat. I tried to escape, and he starts kissing me.

Finally, he lifts his head, pure madness in the depths of his dark blue eyes as he says, "I tested you."

No shit.

"Why?"

"I own you, Angela. Your body. Your soul. Your loyalty, too. I will fuck you… that's your body. I will marry you… that's your soul. And, when you don't take an easy out on what we have together, I'll know I have your loyalty."

"I've only known you four days!"

"You've known me for months," he corrects, nibbling on my throat. With his hand as a collar, keeping my head pressed to the siding of the cabin, I can't escape the warmth of his mouth. It's such a contrast to the chilled rain, I find myself heating up despite my better judgment. "Since you gave me the daisy."

That stupid, stupid daisy.

One last lick and, suddenly, we're moving. Not toward the door, which is what I expected. Instead, he half-shuffles, half-carries me to the makeshift parking space next to the cabin. His SPD cruiser is parked next to an oversized pickup truck.

Using his strength, he bends me over his cruiser,

hiking up the SPD shirt I still have on as high as it goes.

I yelp. The hood of the car is covered in rain, the metal holding the cold more than the cabin siding. It goes right through my shirt, stinging my boobs. They're basically mashed against the hood as Burns forces me to arch my back, my ass sticking out.

"See. I already warned you, angel. Good girls get pleasured, and bad girls? They get punished."

By the time the shirt is bunched around my waist, I've got a pretty good idea what kind of 'punishment' he has in mind.

It's pleasure, all right. It's just pleasure that he's not adding to our little tit for tat arrangement.

I could shout. We're not in the basement anymore, with its soundproofing. And while his cabin is surrounded by trees and hills, there's gotta be someone nearby. Right? Maybe they would hear me. Maybe they would save me.

And maybe, just maybe, I should wait and see exactly what my captor has in store for me.

"What... what are you going to do to me?"

Burns trails a big hand down the back of my bare thigh. His heat scorches me through the chilly rain. "What I've wanted to do since I first met you."

I wiggle, trying to break free of his hold. It's not an act. "You can't," I gasp. "You promised."

He said I could believe him. That if I let him do whatever he wants to me... with his fingers, with his tongue... he wouldn't shove his cock inside of me. He would wait until I wanted it.

Until I begged for it.

Burns's fingers bite into my hips. His body is bowed over mine, pressing me further against the chilly, slick hood. Rain drips from his jaw onto the back of my neck. Despite the two of us being soaked, his heat is like a brand reaching past the clothes clinging to me. And his cock... in this position, he has it nestled against my ass. I can't deny that he's aroused. That he probably orchestrated this whole situation so that I'd try to escape and he could punish me by fucking me for the first time.

From the moment I woke up, cuffed to that cot, I knew that this was in Burns's plan. He said as much himself. He expected me to become his willing wife eventually—and he made it clear he was aching to consummate whatever relationship he'd built up in his head.

Inevitable. It was inevitable. I just... I never thought he'd fuck me outside, in the pouring rain, and only because I fell for his trap.

But he surprises me. Mason fucking Burns. Always full of surprises.

He drops to his knees behind me. "What am I

doing? I'm going to worship my angel the way she deserves to be... with my mouth."

"What?"

A husky laugh sends warm air across my ass cheeks. Hooking a finger beneath my damp panties, he eases the fabric to the side, giving him access to my mound.

"When I take you the first time, when I claim you, it won't be where someone might hear. I told you, angel, your screams belong to me. But that doesn't mean I'm not going to remind you that I also own your pussy. So be a good girl and don't move."

I try not to. Something about his order... he wants me to. And as he begins to eat me out from behind, licking, sucking, and dipping his tongue inside of me even farther than he did last night, I can't help but squirm.

He slaps my ass.

I gasp. On the heels of the sting comes more pleasure than I would've expected.

Burns knows, too. "Move if you want. You'll just get another slap every time you do."

He doesn't make threats, I remember. He makes promises.

I squirm. He slaps me again, and I have to swallow my moan.

"You like that? My pretty little angel... so good, but

you're a bad girl, too, aren't you? You wanted to be punished, didn't you?"

I... I don't know.

He doesn't wait for my answer. With a ferocity that I shouldn't be surprised about by now, Burns makes it his duty to make me squirm again and again. I take the slaps, getting hotter, growing wetter every fucking time his palm makes contact with my ass, and before I know it, I'm coming.

He's not satisfied with me doing it once. Oh, no. As soon as my legs start shaking, he doubles his efforts. The moment I come down from the first climax, I'm almost immediately cresting again.

And he's still not stopping.

"No more," I beg. "I can't take it."

Burns pulls away from my oversensitized pussy. For a heartbeat, I actually believe that he's going to show me mercy. My legs have gone weak. The only things keeping me from collapsing to the wet gravel are Burns's hands on my thighs. In a burst of lust-induced inspiration, I realize what he meant by punishment. This... *this* is my punishment. Orgasm after orgasm with no relief as he fucks me with his tongue, the rain cascading down on us.

And I know I tried to escape him, but right now? I'd be happy to be back in the basement, coming down from the heights of my pleasure somewhere warm and dry without him using my weakness for his touch against me.

As if Burns is inside my brain—and, hell, sometimes I think he *is*—he chuckles, then nibbles one of my ass cheeks. The shock of his teeth biting into my flesh has me moaning, then pleading with him to do it again.

"Oh, angel. It wouldn't be a punishment if I did everything you asked of me. You're mine. Nothing is going to stop me from taking everything I want... and you're going to give it to me."

"But... but I already did. Twice."

"You know what they say." Burns moves back to my pussy. He gives me a long, lazy lick, before telling me, "The third time's the charm."

In that case...

Half delirious with pleasure so intense it's dancing along the edge of being pain, my fingers scrabble against the hood of the cruiser. The rain makes it impossible to get a good hold, but I try anyway as I mumble, "I need—"

"I know exactly what you need," purrs Burns.

He has one finger in. As I push back against him, he works in a second. Just like when he fingerfucked me, I can pretend it's something a little thicker, a little sturdier... I can pretend it's *him*.

Fuck. He was right. That's exactly what I needed.

As the latest orgasm slams into me, I let out a weak

cry. I press my overheated cheek against the metal of the cruiser's hood, searching for some relief. I don't even bother trying to break free of my captor. Burns is playing my body like a goddamn fiddle, ripping every reaction he can out of me.

It was his fingers that did it. To me, penetrative sex —specifically p in v—is the one thing I couldn't agree to. If I did, it was like telling Burns that he owned every inch of me. Still, the way he lapped at my pussy, nibbling on my clit, dipping his tongue inside of me... I needed more. The two fingers he jammed inside my pussy, stretching me out and giving me something to tighten around, was exactly what I needed to come apart beneath him.

I'm done. Feeble as a kitten, he could get off of his knees, shove his pants down around his ankles, and start fucking me here and now—and I would stay just like this and let him.

But he doesn't.

With a husky, amused chuckle, Burns bites gently on my inner thigh. When I whimper but don't react other than that, he chuckles again; this one sounds both satisfied and proud. He rubs his cheek along the back of my thigh, the rain dripping down enough to blunt the rasp of his stubble.

Then, rising up, he reaches around me. I don't resist at all as he tips me into his arms. Burns has one arm under my naked ass, the other supporting my back. It's a typical bridal-style carry—naturally—and he takes advantage of the hold to steal a fierce kiss.

I taste myself as he slides his lips against mine. Rain, too, but mainly my musk as he presses harder, wordlessly ordering me to open my mouth and let him in.

And, God help me, I do.

TWELVE
TRANSACTIONAL

ANGELA

I let him finger me—and he took one of my cuffs off.

He went down on me—and he fed me a slice of my favorite cake.

I tried to escape—and he made me orgasm out in the rain.

I'm not sure what's next for my captor and me. Considering he leaves me as soon as he carries me downstairs—the last thing I expected from him—I think he's leaving me to stew in my own thoughts as the next stage of my punishment.

We had breakfast. I never get lunch when he's at work; no need, since Burns specifically stocked the fridge with my favorites on purpose. I'm wondering if

I'll get dinner or if that'll be another punishment when I hear the locked door creak open again.

Despite it being his day off, when he comes back down to the basement, he's in a fresh uniform. He looks as fresh as a freaking daisy, as though he's ready to head off to work. He's not, though. He's just reminding me—as if I could forget for even a second—that he's a cop, and my jailer.

After my escape attempt, I did figure the second part of my punishment was how he left me all alone. I took the time to take another shower, trading the soaked t-shirt and panties for fresh clothes. The towel I used last night was back in the bathroom. I put my hair up with it until it was dry enough to try to tame the worst of the tangles with my fingers.

He brought my clothes. Still no hairbrush, damn it.

But when Burns comes downstairs, something's different. As cold as I was out in the rain, he's even colder. His jaw is firm, his expression emotionless—at least, until he crooks a finger at me and I get a hint of that charming smile of his.

"Come here, Angela."

Angela. Not 'angel'.

Yup. I'm still in trouble.

Gulping, I get up from the cot. I don't approach him, though. As though he's the big, bad predator and I'm the frightened prey—not too far from the truth, actually—I stay where I am.

For some reason, that amuses him.

"If you don't come to me right now, you'll end up crawling."

I'd rather die. "Why? What are you going to do to me?"

"Oh, no. It's what you're going to do to me."

What?

He pats the bulge in his uniform pants. "It's my turn."

I shake my head. "I didn't scream. You said you wouldn't gag me if I didn't scream."

Burns clicks his tongue. "You did. Did you want my neighbors to hear you? Did you want them to come rescue you?"

Oh my God. He's talking about when I screamed as he was making me come. I wasn't even thinking... it just felt so good, I couldn't help it.

"Burns, that's not... no." Yes? I don't know... "It's not the same."

"That's where we're going to have to agree to disagree. Because I think it is. You screamed, Angela. I told you what would happen if you did. Don't make me a liar and get on your knees." He waits a moment, eyes flashing in barely contained... something. Anger? Lust? Both? "On your fucking knees."

The harsh edge of his voice has me doing just that.

He moves until he's standing right in front of me.

I meet his gaze, then ask, "Are you still punishing me?"

He grips me lightly by the hair, forcing my head back so that I'm staring up at his face from my place on my knees. "Do you think you're being punished, angel?"

I want to tell him to stop calling me that. Angels don't go to their knees this easy, or fantasize about getting trapped by a powerful man and having their pussy devoured in the rain...

Even worse, the truth is, when it comes to whether or not sucking Burns's dick in my mouth is a punishment, I don't know. I just don't fucking know.

I don't have to. Like everything else since he took me, he takes the choice out of my hands.

He fingers the badge pinned to his uniform shirt before dropping his hands to his waist. His gun is strapped in his holster. With his pointer finger, then taps the butt. "You wanted me to do this. Don't deny it."

Damn it. Burns might be a bastard, but he might also be right.

No.

No.

That's the stress of being his captive talking. The sleepless nights, the fear of nightmares returning, the nerves I can't escape, the anxiety that is me wondering what Burns will expect from me next. The flashbacks from that night in Fairview five years ago, and how Brick jumped me for the shop's deposit only a couple of weeks ago.

I don't want to. But this is my punishment, so I will.

Burns can tell.

He smirks. With one quick motion, he releases my hair before reaching for his zipper. He must have already undone the button on his pants because the front peels open as he jerks the zipper down. With no hesitation, he tugs them down. Burns is a boxer briefs man, and I get a glimpse of them before he reaches inside, pulling out his hard cock.

"Forget being punished. This is your reward for being such a good girl."

Reward?

Sucking his dick is *my* reward?

"You don't believe me, do you?"

I believe he thinks so. I believe he wants this almost as badly as me agreeing to let him fuck me. Holding true to his promise, he's not going to *force* me, but he'll cajole and he'll threaten and he'll convince me that doing this is my choice...

He says it's a reward. Maybe... maybe I can make it so.

"I'll do it"—as if I really have a choice—"but only if you do something for me."

His jaw goes tight. His cock bobs, as though reaching for me, but his jaw... he's not happy.

"I don't like our relationship being so transactional, angel."

That's because Burns seems to think we have a relationship that transcends him keeping me in his basement as his prisoner.

"Would you rather force me?" I ask innocently. It's a bluff, we both know it, and I'm actually a little surprised when he doesn't call me on it.

"Never," he answers.

"Then give me what I want. And I'll give you what you want."

"If you want me to let you go—"

I wish. Too bad that that ship has sailed. If I get my freedom, it won't be because he gave it to me. He tricked me once. I'll give him that. I should've known that it was a trap—but he has to mess up for real some time.

I'll be waiting.

Until then...

"I want some entertainment." I can't have my phone, and though I've never been a big fan of social media after what happened to me in Fairview, I doubt he'll let me have a tablet. "A television," I decide. "I want a TV."

"Is that all? I have one upstairs."

I know. I saw it on my way out. "Let me have it. Or

get me one. You promise me that, I'll give you what you want." To prove it, I extend a shaky hand and, wrapping my fingers around his cock, I give him a quick stroke.

He shudders. "Deal."

I keep stroking him. Teasing him. Playing with him the way he played with me even as I nod. "Deal."

Leaning down, he squeezes my jaw just enough to force my mouth completely open, as though desperate to stick his dick inside. That's Burns for you. The moment he gets what he wants, he takes more. I said yes, and he's not wasting a second. As soon as my lips part, he swivels his hips, prodding me with the head of his cock.

"Use your teeth and you *will* be punished."

I one hundred percent believe that.

My tongue darts out, dabbing the head. It's a mixture of salty and tangy, and suddenly, I'm back in that frat house bedroom, a limp dick being shoved in my face.

This dick is hard. It's thicker, too, and it's attached to Mason Burns, not Carter Santorino. I'm still on my knees, though, a position I didn't choose. I'm being told to choke or suck, like I'm nothing but a human fucking fleshlight.

I'm not Angela Havers. I'm a pussy. I'm a mouth.

I'm *nothing*.

And, somewhere over my head, Burns is murmuring, "You want to do this."

He keeps telling me that. Like I wanted him to take me prisoner, and I wanted him to make me come.

I can't make sense of him. One second, he seems to mean it when he tells me that he loves me. The next? I'm nothing but a possession to him. He *owns* me, like I'm some kind of sentient sex doll for him to play with, then put away when he's done for the night.

Does he want me, or was I just convenient? He says he loves me. Twisted as I am, sometimes I'm desperate to believe that, to make sense of what he's done. Then I remember that I'm a loner with no real ties to the neighborhood, I've been gone for days now and I'm not sure anyone misses me.

Why would he want me? It's not like I've ever been anyone's first choice.

Tears well in my eyes. I pretend not to notice them, busing myself instead with running my hand up and down Burns's length. My throat feels tight. I can't bring myself to take more than his head into my mouth, but I continue to play with him, hoping he doesn't realize that I'm struggling.

I should've known better.

Burns notices *everything*.

"Angel... you're crying. Fuck. I... you weren't supposed to cry."

He pulls back, taking his cock with him. Squatting

low enough to reach me, he use his thumb to wipe one of the stray tears settling on the height of my cheek.

Maybe I wasn't supposed to cry. He certainly wasn't supposed to see it.

That doesn't change a damn thing.

I slap his hand away from my face, then grip the base of his cock again. Giving him a squeeze, then a rough stroke, I'm not satisfied until I rip a throaty groan from Burns. When I do, he braces his legs, straight enough to let the feeling skitter up his spine, as he shoves his dick against my palm.

Eyes closed, head thrown back, he's momentarily distracted from my tears.

Good.

I increase the pace. It's not a blowjob, so I'm not floundering in the past. It's just me stroking him off.

That's all.

"Touch me," Burns groans. "Atta girl."

His praise only reinforces my need to take control. The way I feel right now, I'd rip his damn dick off before I let him pry me off of it. He wants release? I'm going to fucking give it to him.

I don't stop working his cock until his big body is bucking, jets of come spurting messily over both of my hands. Only when his chest is heaving, his quickened breath all I hear, do I finally release him.

"Don't forget my TV," I tell him, keeping my tone as cold as possible.

He was right. Transactional is exactly the right word for what we have. I can add giving him a handjob for a television to the list now. At least I learned one thing: if controlling Burns by his cock doesn't work, a couple of tears might.

And since sleeping with him is inevitable, maybe I might be able to barter my freedom for some meaningless sex.

I doubt it—but it's worth a shot.

THIRTEEN
APOLOGY

MACE

I fucked up.

I pushed Angela too far, too fast.

I got cocky. Since it was easier than I expected to convince her to let me touch her, I thought I could do the same thing and get her to show me a little love. A little affection.

A little pleasure.

But trying to order her to give me head? She wasn't ready for that—and I was too selfish to realize that until it was too fucking late.

I made her cry. What kind of worthless monster makes the woman he's obsessed with cry? Even after she realized I took her to make her mine, my angel didn't shed a tear. Not until I made her.

What was I expecting? With her history... I've been careful. No matter what I did, no matter how I pushed her, I recognized that she did have limits. From the moment I promised her I would never force her to do anything with me—or to me—that she didn't want to, I refused to break that promise. I could never get her to stay with me if I forced her to do anything. I knew that.

Until the thought of seeing her lush, pouty lips wrapped around my cock made me forget for one fucking second.

The tears were the slap in the face I needed. Too bad the damage was already done at the cost of my angel's comfort. I didn't get the blow job I was after, though the cold look on her pretty, pretty face as she stroked me to completion made me regret coming at all. I would've killed for my angel to bring me to orgasm... but, instead, I fucked up by doing the one thing I swore I wouldn't.

I'm not heartless. I'm not a fool, either. I know the only reason I've come so far with her is that she believed she could trust me. If I tested her again right now, she'd be gone in a heartbeat, even knowing that she'd be risking my temper—and punishment. I could see it in the way her eyes went cool.

Lying next to her like I have been? Even I know that's out of the question right now.

So once I leave her alone in the basement, I go to my bedroom. That thought playing on a loop in my brain, I open my laptop. One button and the basement fills the screen. I have to make sure that Angela is still there. Though I know there's no way she could've left me, I won't be content until I see it for myself.

For one terrible moment, I think she's gone. Impossible, but it's not like I'm thinking clearly right now. When I can't find her anywhere, my pulse starts thudding, settling only when the bathroom door opens and she appears, drying her hands on her towel.

A pit forms in my stomach. I have no right to be pissed that she washed my come from her hand but, fuck it, I am. Even if I pushed her, the primal part of my masculinity was proud that she carried the scent of my spunk of her. I would've rubbed it in if I thought I could get away with it without making her break.

And she fucking washed it off.

My jaw tightens. I almost want to go back down there and do it again. I know I can't, but the possessive urge is one I've fought against from the second she so innocently offered me the daisy.

Taking a deep breath through my nose, I continue to stare at the screen.

I have five different cameras hidden in the basement. Scrolling through each feed, I settle on the one that gives me the best angle of her as she moves back toward the cot and lays down. As though she knows where they are, she turns her back on the lens. That's okay. The room's wired for sound, too. If she thinks she can cry again and I won't know, she's wrong.

And if she does? I fucking deserve to hear it because, damn it, it's all my fault.

Angela falls asleep long before I even feel tired enough to try.

Like I've done every night for months, I find peace in watching her rest. Just because I'm not sneaking into her apartment to watch her anymore, that doesn't mean I'm going to deprive myself of the one thing that keeps my darker side at bay.

There's only one thing that triggers it. When I was trying to keep my obsession with the pretty little florist on the down low, I couldn't do shit when Angela suffered from her nightmares.

Tonight? When she has the first one since I brought her to my cabin? Nothing can stop me.

She's whimpering, and it's not the good kind. Not like when she first woke up and realized that I'd taken her home with me. That whimper was a promise of what forever with Angela would look like.

This whimper is one of fright that has me tossing the laptop to the foot of my bed before getting up and storming for the basement door.

First the tears, then the nightmares...

I might have caused the tears. And while my actions could have brought the nightmares back, at least those aren't because of me.

I know why she has them. I know everything—except for one thing.

Her eyes are closed, the whimpers reaching me even as I'm standing at the top of the stairs. I take them two at a time, almost tripping in my hurry to get to her. I don't have to be the suave image of Officer Burns she has in her head. I can be the man she wants—the man she needs—and the only one she'll ever have.

I drop to my knees by the edge of the bed. Her whimpers become a frightened moan that has me fisting my hand in fury before I flex my fingers, then stroke her hair.

She jolts.

"Angel," I whisper. "It's okay. I'm here. I've got you."

Her lashes flutter. Half asleep and most likely still trapped in her dream, she jerks her head away from me. "No. Don't touch me."

If I thought she meant me, I'd listen. "Angela..."

She's blinking. Slowly coming to, a wrinkle in her brow I want desperately to kiss away. Finally, she screws up her face, searching for me in the darkness. "Burns?" Her voice is hoarse. "What are... I thought you were... oh my God."

God can't help her, but Mason Burns can.

I get up, sitting on the cot with her. She scoots away from me. I don't like that. Grasping her arm, I tug her so that's right next to me.

"Who made you like this?" I ask her softly. "Who did this to you?"

For as long as I've known what happened to her, I've tried to get the answer to that question. One problem: only two people in the world know who attacked Angela five years ago, and I couldn't ask them. I would've tipped my hand long before now if I commanded my angel to tell me, and the only other person who knew was the bastard who assaulted her.

"Why? Why does it matter? What do you care?"

You know what? It fucking breaks my heart that she's honestly bewildered right now. As though she never thought anyone would want to avenge what happened to her.

I'd say she was still lost in her nightmare if I didn't know better.

Once again, I give her *a* truth.

"I'm the only one allowed to make you scream, angel... and, I promise you, you'll enjoy it every time I do. So, tell me. Who did it? Who hurt you?"

For a moment, I think she's going to deny me. She shouldn't, especially since I was smart enough not to add what I really wanted to: *who do I have to kill?* If she knew what I was planning... my angel would never give up the name.

But she does. On a shaky breath, and with her eyes closed, she whispers, "Carter. His name is Carter Santorino."

I'VE BEEN ON THE JOB SINCE I WAS TWENTY-ONE. AFTER twelve years, I've racked up plenty of PTO. I didn't put in for it immediately after I brought Angela home because I knew I'd need it sooner or later.

Looks like it was sooner.

I take my last scheduled off duty shift to run to the nearest big box store to the hills and get a television for my angel, just like I promised. I have to trust that she'll just use the wireless streaming available on the device to keep herself entertained since there's no cable.

I broke her trust last night. To make up for it, I have to give a little of my own to her as an unsaid apology.

Besides, she's right. I can't expect to win her over if I continue to treat her like a prisoner. I know it's what she wants, but even with my dark side, it seems I have limits, too.

Fuck. I never want to see her cry again. And while I can make sure that I do everything in me to worship my angel and show her that I'm the right man for her, I'm not the only one who hurt her.

She wants me. But the bastard who tried to take what was never his? Five years later, he still haunts Angela.

In that case, it's about fucking time I make him a ghost.

My sergeant knows I do good work. If I need two weeks off for an emergency, he didn't question it. It was a pain in the ass to make sure the patrols were covered, but I offered to do overtime when I get back for some of my brothers, so my leave was approved without any trouble.

Getting my hands on Carter Santorino? That proved to be a little harder.

Unlike Brick, Santorino has money. Well, his dad does. At twenty-five, he's the same age as Angela, and his circumstances are incredibly different. He finished his time at FU and got his degree, though he never left his frat boy-style life behind. Kid's got a rap sheet as long as my arm. Petty theft when he was younger, then plenty of accusations of sexual assault that all seem to get swept under the rug. There are some corrupt cops in Fairview who like Santorino Senior's money.

No wonder Angela never got any justice for the way he attacked her, then threatened her. He ruined her life, then went on his merry fucking way.

Well, not any longer. Not once I can get to him.

It takes three trips to Fairview before I catch him on his own. From the look of him—and the way he's eyeing the woman walking by him on the street—he's trolling for his next target. Whether the woman wants it or not doesn't mean shit to him—or me. Watching the way he licks his lips, then flashes them a plastic smile on his too-handsome face has my skin crawling.

He touched my angel. He tried to force her to do things she didn't want to.

He didn't love her. He just used her.

And now he has to pay.

Too busy looking for a pussy to stick his dick into, he doesn't notice me watching him until it's too late. He doesn't realize that my uniform is a Springfield PD issue and not Fairview, either.

He does see that I'm a cop, though, but only when I'm ready to approach him.

He's watching a long-legged woman with dark hair click-clack down the sidewalk when I move to the left, blocking his line of sight.

A nasty scowl crosses his face. He barely bothers to hide it.

Good.

"Evening, officer. You got a problem or something?"

Ah. The sound of nerves hidden beneath the bravado that comes with thinking you're untouchable. I get that a lot as a cop. I enjoy it, too, especially when

I'm about to prove that no fucking one is untouchable with the right motivation.

He's a dead man walking. He has no clue, but that woman's ass was the last one that he's going to ogle, and the world will be better for it when I'm done.

The revenge belongs to my angel. I could kill him right here, right now, disposing of his body in such a way that no one will ever trace it back to me. As satisfying as that would be for me, Angela needs closure. More than that, he needs to know exactly why death has come for him.

So, instead of making it a quick death, I give him my most charming smile. I tip my cap, shielding the predatory look in my gaze as I shake my head. "Not at all."

He scoffs and starts to pass me by. As he does, I clap him on the shoulder. From the outside, it's a friendly gesture.

At least, until I reveal the injector I had tucked in my palm. One quick jab and I unload the entire sedative into the prick before he even feels the sting of the needle.

It works as quickly on him as it did my angel. I calibrated the dose for his size, his weight, and while his first reaction is to curse at me, then shove me away, it isn't long before he starts stumbling down the sidewalk.

I'm right there, the kind-hearted cop, ready and

willing to offer a shoulder for him to lean on. And when his legs fail, unconsciousness taking him over, I drag him the rest of the way to my truck.

Anyone watching might see a drunk getting a ride home. Just like I planned.

Santorino slumps forward in the cab, head mashed against the dashboard. He's gonna have one hell of a crick in his neck when he wakes up. Of course, that's going to be the least of his worries, especially since I made a pit stop at a florist on my way into Fairview.

It's a four-hour drive back. He slumbers completely unaware through all of it. More than once, I have to resist the urge to open the door and shove him out. For taking advantage of my angel before I was there to protect her, he would deserve it.

I manage to refrain from putting my hands on him until I've parked my truck and unloaded his dead-weight from the cab. Because I couldn't care less what it does to him, I drop him to the ground, dragging him through the mud to the back door.

And since I have to wait for him to wake up anyway, once I get him inside, I decide to finally take some of my frustrations out on the worthless piece of shit.

I move him to the bathroom. It's a lot easier to clean up blood in there.

FOURTEEN
A KIFTSGATE ROSE

ANGELA

When the door to the basement finally opens, I'm surprised by how much I'm looking forward to seeing Burns.

After those two days he was off that we spent together, going back to spending hours upon hours on my own has been hard. The TV Burns brought me helped a little, but it's really just another reminder that I'm by myself. It shouldn't matter. I've been basically alone for as long as I can remember. And yet... I think I can get addicted to the way his attention on me is so all-consuming. Like I matter.

Like I'm the only one who does.

Ever since the nightmares began, though, I've barely seen him. He leaves right after breakfast, and comes back to the cabin well after dark. He won't tell me exactly where I am—he just says it's the hills—but I did get him to tell me that it's an hour's drive from Springfield. Based on how many hours he's been gone, either he's picking up overtime at work—or something else is distracting him.

Maybe even *someone* else...

It's absolutely insane to be jealous that my captor isn't spending time somewhere else. I know that.

Does that stop me?

No. Not even a little.

I jump up, about to cross over to the stairs—

"Why are you doing this? I never did anything to you."

"Shut it," snarls Burns, "or I'll throw you down the steps. Got me?"

"What? You wouldn't dare!"

This is Mason Burns. Of course he would.

The second that thought flashes through my mind, I hear a short scream, followed by a *thump*, and a *thud-thud-thud*. A body comes sliding down on its back, crumpling into a ball as soon as it hits the cement floor.

Burns takes the stairs lightly, shaking his head. "Can't say I didn't fucking warn him. Eh, angel?"

I... I don't know what to say. A hint of humor laces his tone as he comes down, stepping over the groaning mass of male on the floor. I'm glad Burns thinks this is funny.

Me? I'm about to pass out.

Muttering curses under his breath, the man flops from his side to his back. I can see the blond hair matted down with something that turns it unusually dark. The formerly handsome face looks like it's been bashed in. He's covered in injuries too extensive for a shove and fall down the stairs.

Even so, beneath the blood and bruises, I recognize Carter Santorino instantly. How could I not? He's starred in every single one of my nightmares since he assaulted me.

CARTER SANTORINO WAS THE MOST POPULAR GUY WHEN I was an undergrad at Fairview University. Gorgeous and rich, he went through girlfriends like a revolving door. My three years in school, I knew who he was. I knew his reputation. I wished he'd notice me...

...and then he did.

It was at a frat party. Sometimes I think I was a pity invite, the quiet botany student who could only afford to be at FU because I had a scholarship and some loans. Being pretty could open a few doors for me, but those belonging to Psi Omicron's fraternity house weren't one of them until the fateful night one of my female classmates told me I should go.

I did. I had fun, too, until I got corned by Carter Santorino on my way out of the bathroom.

When I first tried to tell anyone else that the infamous Carter assaulted me, there were plenty of witnesses at the party that told me I was begging for it. Asking for it. That I caught his eye early on, regardless of who I was, and the way I paid attention to him as he flirted with me was my signal to him that I was just waiting for him to make his move.

And did he.

In my nightmares, I relive his attack. How he wrapped one hand around my waist, tethering me to him, then shoved his other hand beneath the sweater I was wearing, groping my boob in the empty hallway. When I didn't do anything but stand there, shocked that he had the nerve to just grab me like that, he tightened his hold, manhandling me until I was locked in an empty bedroom with him.

I remember his hands pawing my jeans, breath smelling of beer and cigarettes as he panted in excitement. I kept telling him no, no, I didn't want this, and the fucker forced his tongue in my mouth, then bit my bottom lip before laughing and saying, "Don't give a shit what you want. I'm gonna fuck someone and your pussy is as good as any."

The laugh. The memory of the laugh that

followed sends shivers skittering down my spine even now, five years later. He thought it was funny. He thought it was so fucking amusing, that my worth boiled down to what I had between my legs. All the flirting at the party... it meant nothing. I was just the easy mark he picked up earlier during the party, then waited until he could waylay me on my way out of the bathroom. In the bedroom, it was all about him getting off.

I managed to escape him before it went too far. Luck was on my side that night. He was too drunk to get it up, though he used his grip to knock me to my knees, then shoved his limp cock between my lips. He figured a blow job would get him hard enough to fuck me, and when my terrified licks did nothing for him, he backhanded me.

Even the bruise on my cheek wasn't enough to prove to the cops that he assaulted me. It took every bit of courage I had back then to go to them, and the Fairview police couldn't give a shit.

The name Santorino meant something in the college town.

Havers didn't.

He got off scot-free, a fact he reinforced when he tracked me down two days after my failed police report. Dragging me into a darkened corner of the dorms, he warned me to drop it or he'd finish what he started in that bedroom.

I believed him, too. And I changed my whole life plan to get away from him.

I never thought I would see Carter again. I made it my point. Dropping out of school, running out of Fairview when it became obvious that no one—not my friends, not my fellow students, the dean, the cops... even my own mother—believed me when I said that he forced himself on me.

And that's not entirely true. One girl did. Molly Jacobs, a sweet blonde who was in my Latin class. She believed me because Carter did the same thing to her the semester before.

Only he convinced her that she *did* want it, and only after she slept with him did she realize just how much he forced her. Even when she was telling me in a hushed and frantic whisper about what happened to her, I could tell she still thought she deserved it. That Carter convinced her she was lucky he gave her a ride.

My one big regret in life was that he was free to go after another victim once I made life easy for him and ran away. From Fairview to Bellport, to Plainsborough to Springfield, I've spent five years trying to escape the specter of Carter Santorini.

And I still haven't been able to.

"What... what is he doing here?"

I focus on Burns, then do a double-take. It's him. I'd know that devilish grin anywhere.

I just... I've never seen him in anything but his uniform before.

He's wearing a plain black t-shirt that's probably a size too small; either that, or it's designed specifically to highlight his muscular torso. My eyes are drawn immediately to his forearms, searching out the delicate daisy on such a tough man. He has on jeans, too. I didn't even think he owned a pair.

And sneakers. Dotted with dirt and something suspiciously like blood, Burns has on white sneakers.

He has a black bag hanging loosely from one hand. Whatever he has inside doesn't look too heavy, and there's something pencil-like pushing against the top of the plastic, near the handle.

"Give me a second and you'll see."

Walking over to Carter, Burns kicks him.

Carter groans.

I stare.

Burns kicks him again. "You gonna get up? Or should I drag you again?"

"Fuck you," Carter spits out. "You're the reason my damn arm feels like it's been pulled out of its socket."

Burns shrugs. "Drag it is, then." He tosses the bag at me. "Here, angel. Catch."

A perfect arc, I catch it by the bottom before it falls on the floor. From the familiar feel of something soft, I know exactly what's in there.

Flowers.

What the—

Carter yelps. Using both hands, Burns grabbed one of Carter's, literally dragging his back across the rough floor. When he's opposite of the cot, he flings the former frat boy with enough force to have him spinning, landing flat on his face.

Groaning, he's quick to recover. Shoving off of the ground, he gets to his knees, as though he plans on getting up.

Burns has other plans for him.

With the tip of his sneaker, he flips Carter over again. Once he's down, Burns does the last thing I ever expected him to do.

He quickly pantses Carter, pulling off both the stained jeans he's wearing and the boxers that are underneath. I have no idea what happened to Carter's shoes, but in seconds, he left in nothing but a pair of white socks and a blood-stained shirt.

No matter how much pain he's in, he's quick to cover his dick.

Funny. Last time, he was more than happy to show it off.

"What the fuck, man? What are you doing? I only fuck chicks, not dudes."

Burns's chuckle does something to my insides. "When I'm done with you, you're not fucking anyone, pretty boy." He turns to me, making a grabbing motion with his hand. "Angel? The bag, please."

I have no idea where he's going with this. I toss him the bag anyway.

Once he has it, he points at me. "You recognize her?" When he doesn't answer quick enough, Burns grabs Carter by the hair, jerking his head so that he can't miss me. "Answer the question, Santorino."

Carter's eyes are swollen. Once he realizes that there's no escaping Burns's hold, he blinks slowly, trying to place me. I know in a second when he does.

Bruised and bloody, the bastard can still sneer.

"Yeah. I know her. Fucked her once and she came crying back for more. Shit. Is that what this is about? I didn't give her more dick?"

Liar. He's a *liar*.

And Burns knows.

He *tsks*. "If only that's what this is about. If she'd wanted you, maybe I could forgive what you did to her. But you're not the one who sees her nightmares. Who hears her whimpers. And *that*," Burns says, reaching into the back pocket of his jeans and pulling out a shiny pair of cuffs, "is what this is about."

Moving behind Carter, Burns yanks his arm behind him, snapping the cuff on his wrist. As much as I don't want to see Carter's dick again, I kinda don't have a choice when Burns yanks the other arm even harder. Within seconds, his hands are cuffed behind his back.

He didn't realize what happened until it's too late.

"Hey!" He bucks, his limp dick flapping. Ew. "What are you doing?"

In answer, Burns reaches into the black bag.

"Second question, Santorino. Do you know what this is?" Burns asks Carter.

"I don't fucking know." Howling when Burns wrenches his arm, he pants out, "A flower, okay? It's a flower."

It's not just a flower. It's a kiftsgate rose.

I guess, at first glance, any layman would think it's some kind of basic flower. You know the kind that kids draw? With a yellow circle for a center, then five lopsided petals around it in the same design as a star? One at top, two at the side, and two at the bottom? That's what kiftsgate roses look like. They're persistent little monsters known as a climbing rose because they can climb arbors and gazebos. Most of the flowers grow in bunches, creating wicked barriers made all the more nasty because of their pointed thorns.

Thorns that Burns uses to stab Carter's dick.

Seriously.

Bending down, he grips one of the stems in his hand, pressing it into Carter's naked groin.

With his hands cuffed behind him, the most he can do is throw back his head and howl again, thrashing his legs as Burns squeezes.

The thorns will be tearing into his cock. No doubt about that. Ripping the skin, leaving holes where

Burns is forcing it into Carter's delicate flesh. At the same time, there's no way it isn't doing the same to Burns's palm. When blood starts to trickle down his hand, past his wrist, drip-dropping onto the cement floor, I can only imagine the damage he's doing.

His expression is pure stone. As Carter shouts obscenities that only the three of us will ever hear, Burns keeps one hand on Carter's shoulder, the other holding the thorny stem in place.

It's torture. For both of the men, there's no denying it's absolute torture—and, I realize with a jolt, Burns is doing this all for *me*.

Carter stops screaming long before Burns decides to stop using the thorns of the kiftsgate rose against him. Only when he seems content to wrench every last shout out of the man who assaulted me does the unhinged cop take his bloody hand back.

Leaving Carter quietly sobbing, his head bowed as he makes gasping, animalistic sounds, Burns reaches in his other back pocket.

That one had his gun.

He's wearing a look of pure pride—and that familiar daring smile of his—as he walks over to me and holds out the weapon with his uninjured hand.

"Go on, baby," he says, encouraging me with the glint in his steely blue eyes, and the curve to his lush upper lip. "Even angels can sin a little."

Holy shit. "Me? You want *me* to do it?"

"No." He presses the cool, heavy handle against my palm, folding my fingers over it so that I don't drop the gun on the floor. "*You* want to do it."

You know what? He's... he's *right*.

When the nightmares became too much, I replaced them with fantasies of what I would do if I ever got the chance to confront Carter again. If I wasn't so scared, if pesky little things like right or wrong didn't matter... I wanted to kill him.

I wanted him *dead*.

And this is my chance.

Before I even think twice about what I'm about to do, I lift the gun. It's heavier than I thought it would be. It's notably different from the one that Burns always wears in its holster, too. A personal weapon, I'm betting, instead of his standard issue.

Of course. As insane as Burns is, even he wouldn't use his professional piece to commit murder... right?

Because that's what this is. If I pull the trigger, if I shoot Carter Santorino, it's murder.

And I'm beginning to think I'm just as fucked up as Burns because you know what?

I honestly don't care.

He stole my innocence. My dreams. My *life*.

Well... turnabout is fair play, isn't it?

Planting my feet on the floor, ignoring the way my arms tremble and shake, I take a deep breath and squeeze the trigger.

Carter's head shoots up. "Fuck! Fuck, shit, *fuck*! You shot me! The bitch fucking *shot* me!"

I did, but I missed.

I fucking *missed*—and he's not dead.

Worse, I shot him but it's basically a flesh wound. It's a good thing that he's still cuffed because that means that Carter can't do anything but slam back on the cement floor and writhe as blood gushes from the hole I just shot in his shoulder.

Oh, wait—

He *can*.

In between his panting and his yells, Carter curses me like I'm the devil himself. As dazed as I am, I notice he doesn't use my name once which only reinforces my suspicion that he lied to Burns. Despite starring in every single damn nightmare I've had for the past five years, the bastard has no clue who I am. To him, I'm just another pretty face in a long line of girls he tried— and often succeeded in—to fuck, whether she wanted it or not.

It's the fury in Carter's tone that has me frozen in place. That, and the stink of gunfire in the air and the way my ears are ringing just beneath his shouts. I don't know what else to do but stand there and take his abuse as the gun hangs limply from my tingling hand.

With Carter swearing all the terrible things he's going to do to me next, the idea to lift the weapon again and finish the job never even crosses my haze-filled mind.

Luckily for me, it does my captor's.

Easing the gun out of my loose grip, Burns aims and he fires. There's no hesitation as he angles his arms just so to shoot Carter dead in the chest. The heart, I think, because apart from a single gasp before he jerks once, he stops moving.

Carter shuts up, too, which was probably the point considering Burns says coldly, "You shouldn't have called her a 'bitch'," as he stalks over to the corpse, giving it one last kick before checking the safety on his gun.

Once he's sure the weapon is safe, he pockets it again, then moves away from Carter before turning to me.

I'm gaping over at him.

I... I don't know how to react. Instinctively, I want to go to him—to go to my captor and my savior, seeking comfort and safety and I'm not so sure what else—and because it's the single thing I can think to do, I do it.

It's only as Burns pulls me into his arms, stroking my back as my trembling hands turn to full-body tremors, that it hits me that I never even thought to turn the gun on him while I had the chance.

FIFTEEN
REWARDED

ANGELA

Burns takes care of the corpse.

He waits until I'm steady enough to pull out of his arms on my own before he tells me to sit down. Wordlessly, I obey him. Dropping my head in my hands, I peek through the slivers in my fingers as he hefts Carter's body off the floor and disappears up the steps with him.

I don't know how long he's gone. It feels like no time at all, though I'm sure it has to be an hour or more at least. I busied myself by gathering the scattered rose petals on the floor and trying to salvage as much of the flower that I can. A sick part of me wants to press it between the pages of my botany book, a memento from this dark night.

Because I like the idea of doing that far too much, I force myself to toss them into the garbage pail.

The blood spray covering the floor has got to go, too, I decide, and I do my best to clean it up.

I go back to the cot when I hear the door to the basement open again. The second I plop down, I realize that I'm too wound up to sit, so I'm standing again as Burns reappears.

There's a mess of blood on his hands, on his t-shirt, all over his once-white sneakers. Dirt, too. A smear covers his cheek, highlighting just how dangerous he appears right now.

Or maybe that's the gun he has in his hand again.

I swallow the lump lodged in my throat. Taking a step toward him, I pause when he stops at the base of the stairs. "Is everything—"

Look at me. I can't bring myself to say it.

I don't have to.

"It's taken care of. You okay, angel?"

I nod. "You?"

Something's different about Burns. Like a powder keg about to explode, I can sense him thrumming in place, as though one spark is going to set him off. He's not usually like this. That's one thing I can say. For good or for bad, what I see is what I get with him. If he's holding something back, there's a reason.

And I'm not so sure I want to know what it is.

He obviously doesn't want to discuss what just

happened. Maybe it's because he's gauging my reaction, waiting for me to fall apart. I mean, I did just witness him torture and execute Carter Santorino right in front of me—and that was after I shot a gun for the first time in my life.

Yeah. It's probably that one.

Only... I'm not about to. I wasn't lying. When I said I was okay, I meant it. Sure, I could be better, but I have to look at the bright side: Carter is dead. *Gone.* Burns killed him, and I'll never have to worry about that bastard coming after me again.

Though I do have to accept that he probably never would have. For God's sake, he didn't even recognize me when Burns threw him at my feet.

Does that change a thing about how I feel right now? It should... but it doesn't.

However, Burns is eyeing me closely as though expecting me to act a totally different way than I am. I might as well give him *something.*

Gesturing vaguely at him, I ask. "Shouldn't you... I don't know... clean up?"

I'll be honest. The blood *is* making my stomach twist. Just not for the reason I want him to think...

Because the real truth is that, ever since I've been here with Burns, I'm different. I'm changing. I'm... I'm *glad* that Carter is dead. All I ever wanted was someone to take his assault on me seriously, and to make him pay. The cops in Fairview didn't do shit.

But Burns... he gave me the chance to get vengeance myself. When I couldn't, he did it for me.

The blood doesn't disturb me. It *excites* me. And since that fact *does* disturb me, I need him to give me some space. Before I do something I regret. Before he *does* explode. Before I dwell too closely on tonight's events... I need some space.

Only I don't think I'm getting any.

Still clutching the gun, he grabs the hem of his blood-stained t-shirt, tugging it over his head and tossing it to the floor. "That better, angel?"

Oh. Um. Coming face to face with Burns's bare chest for the first time... I wasn't expecting that, either. This is the most I've seen of him and, without meaning to, I stare again.

I might've got a glimpse of his chest once when he came down with his uniform shirt halfway undone. This, though? This is an idea of what he'll look like when he finally takes me in his bed.

When...

If. I mean *if.*

Don't I?

I don't know anymore.

"I—" I give my head a clearing shake. Forcing myself to look away from his hairless chest and a set of gorgeous pecs, I drop my gaze to his palms. "There's blood on your hands," I say needlessly.

"I know."

"Aren't you going to wash them?"

"I will," he bites out, his voice short and his eyes... glancing up, the steely blue shade of his eyes is darker than I've ever seen. "As soon as I get my reward."

His *what*?

I finally meet the daring look on his darkly handsome face. "What are you talking about?"

"You owe me."

Tit for tat.

As I stare up at him, he says almost conversationally, "Would it scare you if I told you that I've killed for you before? That that asshole wasn't the first time?"

No. And it wouldn't surprise me, either.

"Burns—"

"My name is Mace."

I know. And since he insists on calling me 'angel' instead of my name, he's 'Burns' to me. "What are you saying?"

"That there's a reason you never heard anything else about your case. The robbery."

Brick. "You killed him?"

"I did. Wanted to kill that prick who tried to steal you from me, too. If I hadn't gotten to you before he could, I might've."

Dean. "Why are you telling me this?"

"Because you need to know what kind of man loves you. You weren't scared before, but when I mentioned the prick... would you like it if I spared him?"

Spared him? I don't... it was one date. One stupid, little date. But Burns... he's serious. He's looking for a reason to go after Dean. I gave him one with Carter, and he used the robbery to go after Brick, but Dean?

"He didn't do anything wrong—"

"Didn't he? I told you before, I won't let anyone come between us. He tried once. What if he tries again? What then, Angela?" When I don't answer him, his blue eyes darken even more noticeably. "What will you do for me if I let him go? Hm?"

I stay silent.

He doesn't like that. "Get on your knees."

I've had enough. "Why are you acting like this? Burns—"

A muscle ticks in his jaw.

"I'm not forcing you to do anything. It's your choice, angel. Something's going in that pretty mouth of yours. Either my gun or *me*."

He's so cold. So calculating. The tender emotion he showed as he held me before is gone. He says he's not forcing me, but with the same gun that shot Carter in one hand, the other yanking down his zipper, pulling out his already hard cock... what kind of fucking choice do I really have?

But maybe... maybe it's not about my choice at all.

I think about how he mentioned 'reward' like that and a lightbulb goes off.

Is that how it is? Just when I start to think that Burns isn't such a monster, that he actually—in his twisted way—*cares* about me, he reduces this thing between us into another transaction. Another trade.

He gave me Carter, he's sparing Dean, so now I have to give him head? That's it, isn't it?

Okay. Fine.

At the very least, if that's all he wants for freeing me from Carter, I'll do it.

As I approach him, I'm careful to keep my head turned away from the spot where Carter died. That's not so difficult. Absolutely sure that he's getting his way in this, Burns starts to take off his pants. As he shimmies his jeans down past his ass, I see that he's gone commando. I have no clue if he does that normally or if he went without underwear because this was always his plan. It doesn't matter. The only thing that does is how quickly his erection springs free, head pointing toward the ceiling once it's allowed out of the confines of his jeans.

A bead of pre-come is already waiting for me on the tip.

I don't realize I stopped moving to stare at his cock until Burns rasps, "Come here, angel. Come closer."

I shuffle the rest of the way toward him. When he's within arm's reach, I sink down in front of him. Going right to my knees, his cock at my eye level, I'm almost... eager to worship him with my mouth.

Especially since he's teasing me by touching himself already.

I'm pretty sure he used his left hand to torture Carter with the rose thorns. He uses the same one to stroke himself. I'll admit, something about seeing his big hand wrapping around his hard cock, pumping it slowly like a gun being primed has my mouth watering—and that's not the only part of me that's wet.

This wasn't my idea. Being intimate with Burns in the room where Carter died... in a million years, I never would've thought I'd get turned on by the idea of going down on a guy, especially after what I experienced tonight.

But Burns isn't just any guy, is he? He's my cop, and there's something truly wrong with me that I'm actually kind of looking forward to tasting him.

My tongue darts out, lapping at my bottom lip. I can feel my eyes going heavy-lidded, an unfamiliar lust coming over me.

Burns lets go of his cock. In a throaty voice full of disbelief, he asks, "You're really going to do it?"

Why wouldn't I? "You told me to."

"I did. I want you to." He pauses, another muscle ticking in his jaw. "*You* want to."

He always seems to think so.

I shrug. Tossing my hair over my shoulder, I reach for him. Might as well get this over with. I need sleep, and I'm already hoping like hell that, with Carter's death, my nightmares have died with him.

But, before I can take his dick in my hand, Burns angles his hips back just enough that I miss him.

"Tell me you love me," he grates out.

What does love have to do with me going down on him?

"Why, Burns?" I ask, holding my own emotions back. "It's just a blow job. Your reward, remember?"

A shadow passes across his face. "It's not, angel. Not with you. Now tell me you love me."

I thin my lips.

"Damn it, Angela." Burns lifts his hand. The gun is aimed right at my forehead. "I killed for you. I'd *die* for you. You're my goddamn world, the only thing worth anything in this life. I love you. You love me. Now fucking *tell* me."

I freeze, staring up at him. I barely even notice the barrel of the gun. I'm just looking at Burns.

Is that what he wants from me? To make me go to my knees in front of him is one thing. But to demand that I tell him something I don't think I can ever mean?

I'll give him my mouth. After what he did for me with Carter, he might even have my loyalty.

He has a long way to go if he thinks he has my heart.

So, without breaking our stare, I jut my chin at him. "You won't shoot me."

I've never been more sure of anything in my life— and Burns knows it, too.

"You're right." He repositions the gun, the barrel kissing his temple. "But what if I shoot myself? I told you, angel. I'll die for you. You want me to prove it?"

My breath catches.

No.

Okay. Burns is insane. In so many ways, he's proven that over and over again since he took me captive. He's insane if he thinks he can make me love him just because he wants me to, and he's insane if he thinks that the intimacy we've shared has anything to do with how I feel about him.

It was tit for tat. It was a trade.

I thought he understood that.

But as he keeps the gun to his head, finger ghosting over the trigger, I'm absolutely positive that my captor would rather kill himself at this moment than go on believing that I don't love him.

What will I do if Burns dies? The thought is so unfathomable I do the only thing I can.

Clutching his nearest thigh, digging my nails into the muscle, I yell, "I love you!" just like he wants.

He keeps the gun in place, finger hovering over the trigger. "Then suck me off like you mean it."

For both of our sakes, I do.

I immediately grip Burns's cock by the base, sucking the head in between my lips before he can do anything we'll both regret. When he moves his hips, trying to pull back, I refuse to let him. He wants me to suck him? I will, and we'll both deal with the consequences of his order later.

Even after he lowers his hand, letting the gun fall to the ground with a clanking sound, murmuring that I called his bluff, that I don't have to do this unless I choose to, I don't stop until he's bucking into my mouth, filling me with his come.

I've never swallowed before. With Carter, it never got that far. I'd taken a couple of my other boyfriends in my mouth, always spitting because the idea of willingly swallowing their jizz used to skeeve me out.

With Burns? I swallow every fucking drop and hope like hell he's happy now.

SIXTEEN

THE BAD GUY

ANGELA

Once he finished, Burns disappears into the bathroom, returning a few seconds later with a cup of tap water in his hand.

He holds it out to me. "Drink."

I grab the cup, swallowing just enough of the water to rinse out my mouth, then spit it on the floor after swishing it around.

Some of it splashes on his muddy sneakers.

Good.

Burns makes an amused sound in the back of his throat. "I guess, if it's a choice between you spitting my come or the water, it makes me happy knowing you swallowed straight from my cock."

Does he have to put it like that? So I did. In the

heat of the moment, I sucked every last drop of him I could get, as though I could get him to put the gun away by the power of my mouth on his dick alone.

Burns gets one look at my face and, just like that, his amusement is gone. It's like a fucking switch, how quickly he can go from one mood to the next. Instead of teasing, he's suddenly serious, looking down at me with an expression so different from the cold one he gave me as he ordered me to go to my knees.

I hate it. I fucking hate it. I don't know which one is the real Burns. The protective hero who did what the other cops couldn't, finally bringing Carter to justice, or the insatiable lover who obviously knows my history as a SA survivor and still pushes me farther and farther than anyone else ever has before?

What about the nice guy cop? The bad guy captor? The broken, obsessed man who saw something in me he wanted and *took* me because of it?

I don't know. I'm not sure I'll ever know.

He killed Carter for me, then decided his reward was to make me get on my knees. How is that any different than what Carter did to me? So far I've managed to convince myself that letting him touch me, kiss me, taste me... those were things Carter wouldn't have done. He just wanted to stick his dick in me, whether I wanted him to or not.

But Burns... it was never about him getting off until tonight. I might've stroked him off once before, but *I* made that choice. I took ownership in that moment.

Did I have any tonight?

I want to believe that, if I held firm and refused, Burns would've backed off. He swore he would never force me, but he never said he wouldn't manipulate the circumstances so that I'd say yes because saying no wasn't really an option.

Like, say, when he has a gun to his head...

I still can't believe he did that. Threatening Dean... that's something I'd expect from him. Me going on that date with him is what set my cop off in the first place. He thought I was choosing another man and decided to take the choice out of my hand by making me his personal prisoner.

I never doubted for a moment that he could point a gun at me all day long and never shoot it. But when he pointed it at himself? I don't want to examine too closely *why*, but that... that did something to me.

And why did he do that? Because he wanted me to finally get on my knees for him?

Without meeting his gaze, I hand the half-drank cup of water back to Burns. He takes it, and I wordlessly turn my back on him.

I tried my best to clean up the blood spatter on the cement floor while Burns was taking care of Carter's body, but without bleach, I could only do so much. I purposely avoid looking at the part of the basement, instead heading right over to the cot.

I lay down on my side. A second later, the cot dips, Burns stretched out behind me.

Because of course he is.

He sighs. "Fine. Be angry at me all you want. So long as you're not angry at yourself."

Of all the emotions running through me right now, anger at myself isn't one of them.

"Why would I be?" I mumble at the wall.

"Because of that prick who attacked you. He deserved everything he got tonight, and you deserved to witness it. He can't hurt you anymore."

"He can't," I retort, suddenly as angry as I denied I would be. "But what about you?"

Burns kisses the back of my neck. "I won't. I swear I won't."

How can he honestly think I believe that? After what he just did?

And I'm not talking about his demanding head. The transactional side of our... whatever we have... makes it so that we have some kind of balance between us. Technically, he's in control. Of course he is. He has the cuffs, the gun, the badge, and the lock on the door. He has my freedom in his hands.

But he also plays with me, letting me think I have *some* power.

Carter didn't care what I wanted. Burns insists I

want everything he does to me—and maybe what happened five years ago really fucked me up because, damn it, I *do*. Something about the way he takes the choice out of my hands while also ensuring that I'm pleasured... that I'm not just used... is so different from my assault that, except for the last time Burns wanted me to blow him, I could keep the two separate.

Until tonight. Until he went a step too far with the gun.

The revelation that Burns is a killer isn't a surprise. Neither is finding out that he's the reason Brick disappeared.

But how can he swear that he'll never hurt me after the stunt he just pulled?

"Burns... you pulled your gun on me. You said you'd never hurt me, and you threatened to shoot me."

"No, I didn't."

I stiffen. If there's one thing I hate more than anything in this world, it's someone gaslighting me. I was there. I know what he did. He can't tell me that he didn't *when I was fucking there.*

I don't get the chance to argue. Before I can, Burns notices my reaction and says, "Believe me, angel. I would never put a gun to your head with a loaded chamber."

His weight on the tiny bed shifts. I can't see what he's doing behind me—and I'm stubborn enough not to look—when, suddenly, he's back. He must've reached over the edge of the cot to retrieve his gun because he leans over me now, showing off the open barrel where I can see it.

He's right. The chambers are empty.

Was he fast enough to remove the rounds before he showed me the gun? Maybe.

I have to ask. I have to know.

Finally glancing over my shoulder, I say, "What about you? What about the way you put the gun to your temple like that?"

Burns disappears the gun. I don't know where he puts it since I'm not looking at his hands. Oh, no. I'm completely distracted by the determined look on his face and the solemness that thrums in his tone as he admits, "If I thought I would lose you, I wouldn't fucking hesitate to pull the trigger."

Oh.

I let that sink in for a minute. If he's telling the truth, that means that Burns would rather blow his own brains out than live without me and... yeah.

I don't know what to say to that.

My whole life, I've never had anyone who cared about me that much. I still don't know what I did to make it so that Burns does. The only thing he said was that, from the moment I gave him that first daisy, I was his—even if I didn't know it yet. He picked me out because I was kind to him, just like I admired him from afar because he was handsome, he seemed strong, and he saved me from danger, something none of the cops back in Fairview ever did.

At that moment, when Burns turned the gun on himself... that was the first time I've felt fear—real fear —since I woke up in the basement and realized I was trapped. Somehow, in the time since he stole me, I stopped being afraid of him. He promised he wouldn't force me to do anything I didn't want to. I've held him to that.

But when I believed he was going to shoot himself, I *was* afraid. And maybe most of that was because I'd be stuck in the basement with the body of a dead cop, but a tiny part of me was terrified to see Burns blow his head off.

Did I really think he would? No.

Was I thinking rationally? Not even a little.

And to hear him admit that it's something he wouldn't hesitate to do in certain circumstances... I simply don't know how to respond to that.

So I don't. Instead, I ask, "If the gun wasn't loaded, then why do it at all?"

"Because I know you, angel. You've been dying to get your mouth on my cock, but you're just too *good*. You wouldn't go down to your knees on your own, but if I gave you a reason to? If I gave you the excuse? I'd get inside of you one way or another, and you can continue to think of me as the bad guy."

I look away from him, staring at the cinderblocks

again as I tell him honestly, "You *are* the bad guy, Burns."

Another kiss on the back of my neck. "I know. And you love it." His hand squeezes my hip, a possessive brand I can't ignore. "Ain't that right, angel? You love me."

My panicked voice echoes in my ear. *I love you!*

"Don't get any ideas." Hiding my embarrassed flush, I'm mumbling into my pillow. "I only said it because of the gun."

Silly Angela. I should've known better than to think that Burns would let me get the last word, especially now.

Rising up on his elbow, he leans over me, gripping my chin and turning my face so that I can't continue to hide from him. Then, once he has me right where he wants me, he kisses me. A deep kiss that has me forgetting myself as I turn the rest of the way into him, my fingers clutching at his bare chest as I gasp into his mouth.

When he finally breaks the kiss, his lips curve into a knowing grin. "Lie all you want. I know better, baby, and they still taste fucking delicious."

But I'm not lying.

I'm *not...*

...right?

I LOSE TRACK OF HOW LONG WE LAY TOGETHER LIKE THIS. With one of Burns's arms tucked beneath me, the other thrown over my side, tugging me so that my front is nestled comfortably against his bare chest, I'm too cozy to move.

Besides, even if I do turn away from him, he'll just spoon me from behind. I can't get away from him, and hours after Carter Santorino died in front of me, I realize I don't want to.

Does that mean I want to stay in this basement?

I... don't.

It's not like I believe in ghosts. That's not it at all. I keep waiting for some kind of remorse to hit me that, because of me, a man is dead. I *shot* someone, and I watched him be tortured before he died.

And all I feel is a sick sense that justice was finally served.

How many future victims did I save? That's the way I keep looking at it. If the number is even one, I can't bring myself to feel bad about what happened to him.

But that's the thing. Knowing the lengths that Burns will go to make me happy? Because, to my cop, that's exactly what he was doing when he went after Carter... and with that, something's changed between us. Even if I wasn't so sure about that, the way he successfully manipulated me into going down on him proves it.

Because he was right. Deep down, I wanted to do it. He just gave me the excuse.

He made himself the bad guy, and while there's no denying he *is*, I'm not a victim. Not anymore.

And I'm ready to get the hell out of this basement.

Burns isn't a mind-reader. Sometimes I'm terrified that he is. He knows so much about me. My thoughts. My memories. My motives. I mean, he knew about Carter. I never told another soul about him after no one believed me the first time, but Burns already knew that *someone* had hurt me before I ever confessed his name, unwittingly signing my attacker's death warrant.

Just like Brick. He's dead because of me, and I... I don't care. If Burns went after Dean, I might. He's an innocent in all this, a chess piece who never even knew he was on the board. Now he was nothing but a pawn to use against my captor—only Burns ended up using Dean against me instead.

I thought I knew him. Officer Burns. I thought I did.

I'm learning that he's nothing like what I believed... and that could mean big, big trouble for me.

I can't sleep. Not for fear that the nightmares will find me, but because I don't think I can spend one more night as his captive. From this moment on, I consider myself his partner in crime.

It's time I started to act like it.

He's not sleeping, either. Despite my head buried against him, listening to his steady heart and his soft, panting breaths, I know that he's as wide awake as I am.

Then he murmurs, "You okay, angel?," and I know I'm right.

Before, when he asked me that, it was in that emotionless voice he uses sometimes when he's not sure what kind of reaction he'll get from me. Now? That seductive warmth, the same cajoling tone he often uses when he wants me to fall apart in his arms... it's back in his voice.

Burns is back. *My* Burns.

I sigh. "As good as I can be."

"You haven't slept yet. You need your rest."

"I know. I'm trying."

"So what's the matter?" He pauses before murmuring into the darkness, "Do you regret what we did?"

We. See? Partners in crime, just like I thought.

I think about what he said for a moment. I could lie to him, but he'll know. Then Burns would probably take the excuse to kiss me again, to call me out on thinking I could fool him. Why not just cut to the chase and tell him the truth for once?

"I regret missing," I confess. "I regret you having to finish him off because I couldn't."

"You did more than enough—"

I shake my head, burying it deeper into Burns's chest. He smells so good, it isn't fair. A twisted part of me thinks it's the scent of blood—Carter's blood—clinging to his skin that's so enticing. It's not just that, though. Burns's innate scent is intoxicating: woodsy, dark, and undeniably dangerous. "You shouldn't have killed for me."

"Wasn't the first time," he reminds me.

Right. And that's something else I'm still trying to process. "Carter was my problem."

"He was. But your problems are my problems, angel. Haven't you figured that out yet? You're mine, and I take care of what's mine. I'm still pretty fucking impressed with your shot, though. For the first time firing a gun, you did good, baby." He strokes the back of my head, fingers running through my hair. "I always knew you had a bit of devil in you. Just enough to make you my perfect match. My perfect soulmate."

My heart skips a beat. When I first discovered the depths of Burns's obsession, a statement like that would frighten me. Now? I'm just confused because I'm not feeling scared right now. I don't know what it is, but it's not fear.

No surprise, he *knows.*

He knows fucking *everything.*

"Ang... there's something else. Something you're not telling me."

I nod, my forehead bumping into his sculpted pec

before I shift my position, laying my cheek against it. "I want to leave the basement," I whisper.

It's Burns's turn to sigh. "I can't let you go. I wouldn't have anyway, but after tonight—"

Right. Tonight, when Burns made himself vulnerable by committing murder right in front of me. And if he's not vulnerable, then I'm a fucking target. No way he'll risk me running off and telling anyone what I saw.

Of course, given my track record with making police reports, they'll never believe me. Doesn't mean I'm not a loose end that he might be forced to tie up one day.

Then again, if I'm stuck in his basement forever...

"You got me wrong. I don't want to leave the cabin." Shit. I don't want to leave *him*... and I don't know what that says about me right now. "But I can't stay in this room anymore."

He drops his hand, caressing the side of my throat. "Oh. In that case... yeah. Sure. If that's what you want, angel, we can head on up to my bed."

The Burns I'm used to would take the chance to lord my request over me. He'd point out that he always knew he'd get his way. That me willingly joining him in his bed is one step away from what he's been after all along: fucking me and making me his.

In the quiet of the late night, he doesn't do that. He

simply holds me close, waiting for me to give the signal that I'm ready to go.

And it hits me. Something's changed all right... but it isn't just me.

In case I'm imagining it, I pull away from him enough so that I can look him in the eyes. "Don't you want me to beg?"

I'll never forget my first day down here. When Burns told me this was my room until I begged him to let me move into his. Since he's spent every night since the nightmares came back with me, the basement basically turned into his room, but I know he has an actual bedroom somewhere else in the cabin.

"There are plenty of times I will. Not denying that. Sometimes, though... hearing you ask me so sweetly is even better than when you plead."

Ah. There's the Burns I know and—

Know.

SEVENTEEN

DINNER WITH BURNS

ANGELA

The bed in Burns's room is a queen. Compared to the cot I've been sleeping on since he's brought me to his cabin, it's *massive*. There's certainly more than enough space for the both of us.

So why do I wake up snuggled up against Burns?

Him being right there isn't unusual. Apart from my first night here, he's found an excuse to join me in bed every time I go to sleep. Even when he gave me my space after the whole blowjob incident, he came back as soon as the nightmares found me. Since then, he hasn't bothered with pretending that he doesn't plan on spending every single free moment he has at my side.

His patrol schedule is pretty regular. I figured it out

when he was patrolling outside of the flower shop where I used to work. As a cop, he has five-on, two-off one week, then four-on, three-off the next. His shifts range from eight to ten hours depending on the week, though if he's behind on paperwork or decides to take advantage and rack up the overtime, they can be longer.

Burns had his usual days off last week. I thought he was working all along this past week, though that got shot to hell when he confessed he had spent days stalking Carter before he could bring him to me so that we could 'enact our revenge' on him. Because of that, I was convinced he'd be going back to work today, even if I was kind of also waiting to see what his next move would be.

I got to sleep in his room last night. No doubt in my mind he found a way to lock us in, but if he goes back to work today, what then? Do we go back to how it was? Or does Burns realize that—no matter how I tried to fight it—everything has changed?

And when he wakes up, one hand thrown over my waist, pulling me up against his hard body, his husky chuckle and quick admission is how I find out about his vacation.

Turns out that it started three days ago. He wasn't sure how long it would take for him to get to Carter so he put in for two weeks off in case it took longer than he expected. With all that behind us—and an obvious erection behind *me*—that means, for another week and a half, I have Mason Burns all to myself.

It also isn't that long before I realize that, yes, Burns can tell the difference in how we were before Carter and now. For the first time since he grabbed me, he's not treating me like his prisoner.

I'm his lover. His partner.

And if he has his way, I'll be his *wife*.

My obsessed cop hasn't given up on that idea. When he finally relents and allows me to call my mom, he promptly takes the phone out of my hand and introduces himself as my fiancé. He doesn't give Mom any other information than that. Not his name. Not his occupation. Just that I'm his before he smirks at the way my jaw dropped, then presses my phone back against my palm.

Burns is smart. He knows exactly what he's doing, too. My relationship with my parents became strained after my assault. That's partly my fault—me blaming my parents for not being able to make the situation better—and theirs, since they believed the police when they shrugged their shoulders and said I wasn't a victim.

I call my parents twice a year: on my birthday and Christmas. That's the extent of the relationship I want to have with them, so me calling suddenly with news that I'm engaged wouldn't be out of the realm of possibility.

Of course, I can't flat-out deny Burns's claim without having to explain the *real* situation. Like I'm ever going to do that. In one fell swoop, he ensures that my parents know I'm safe, believe I'm in a loving relationship, and that there's a chance I won't want to call them again for fear of discussion details about a wedding that I'm stubbornly insisting will never happen.

Calling me his 'good girl' when I reluctantly tell my mother that he's my partner—which, okay, at least that's a *little* true... and it's a hell of a lot better than saying he's my lover—Burns decides it's time for another reward.

And, whoa. This one's a doozy.

———

EXCEPT FOR MY FAILED ESCAPE ATTEMPT OUT INTO THE RAIN, I haven't left Burns's cabin since the day I entered it. That's why I'm so surprised when, a couple of days after I moved into his bedroom with him, he brings the skimpy red dress up from the basement.

Hanging it on the door, he shuffles me into the master bathroom. The whole cabin itself is super rustic. Masculine, too. Shades of brown fill the place, and when I teasingly point out that it lacks a woman's touch, Burns takes my hand, kisses the back of it, and tells me I can do whatever the fuck I want to it.

It's *our* home, after all...

He bought it years ago, I found out, but not for any reason other than the fact that—like me—sometimes the city is too much for him. The cabin's become Burns's personal sanctuary. No one else has ever set foot inside. Just me and Carter, and for different reasons, we were both unconscious when we arrived her.

When I bite my bottom lip, my expression asking the question I refuse to vocalize, Burns makes it clear: that means no other women, either.

I hate what it does to my mood to know that. Why should I care who Burns fucked before me? With his dark appetites, I figured there has to have been countless others to fulfill his needs.

To my surprise, he makes it a point over his vacation to convince me that my impression of him isn't quite right. He tells me he hasn't been in a committed relationship in at least five years; like me, they were all flings that never got too serious and ended just as quickly. No other woman had ever caught his attention enough for him to want to stick around—not until I gave him the daisy and unknowingly piqued his interest.

An interest that turned into a full-blown obsession before leading to my captivity within just a few of months...

He watched me for all that time. Almost from the

beginning, he decided I was meant for him. That I was the only woman he'd ever want. Aware enough to know what kind of man he really is, he actually tried to stay away at first so he wouldn't scare me.

Of course, then I "flaunted" my date with Dean, making Burns believe he was losing me to someone else. So long as I wasn't with another man, he was willing to keep his distance. The second he thought I was going to sleep with someone else, I triggered the possessive side of my obsessed stalker.

Because, in his kinder moods, Burns repeatedly tells me that he loves me. Sooner or later, he says, I'll love him back. I pushed his hand, and now he's only giving me what I want... at least, that's his opinion on my captivity.

Me? I'm not so sure about that.

I don't doubt that his obsession is definitely *something*—so is the way he insists I belong to him—but love? I have a hard time believing that, though I don't argue with him anymore about it. There's no use, and I only get the cold side of my fiery cop whenever I attempt to.

Just like it's not worth arguing about his feelings for me, the same goes for shower time. I might have avoided being so close to a deliciously naked Burns while I was in the basement. Upstairs? It's like he wants to tempt me into giving in and sleeping with him any way he can. Knowing how well-kept and toned his body is, he uses it against me.

And I let him. Not like I really have a choice.

With Burns, I never do...

The master bathroom is huge. At least three times larger than the tiny room below us, I can't use the excuse that it'll be too crowded in the shower for him to join me when two more Burns could fit in there with me, easy. And... well... if he's going try to get me to beg for his cock by taking every opportunity to pleasure me, what's the harm in allowing him to?

It's probably the dumbest thing I've ever done in my whole life, but I... I kind of trust Burns; at least, with my *body,* I do. Despite his constant teasing, his pushing, his attempt to possess me every moment we're together, my captor's held true to his word. He's probably tasted every last inch of me—and I've done the same to him— but sex... penetrative sex... we haven't gone that far yet.

I'm not ready yet. He knows it, too. Just like how he knows that what Carter did to me has left me all screwed up when it comes to sex. I'm still not sure *how* he knows—I guess being a cop comes in handy, even when it comes to researching a crime far out of his jurisdiction—and I don't ask.

Honestly? I'm afraid to find out what else he knows about me.

One thing for sure, I'm learning things about

myself in his cabin in the hills that I've never known before, either.

Though I'd never admit it to another soul, I actually sort of like it when Burns takes control. It helps that I've seen how easily he's willingly to pass it back to me when I want it, but when he just *takes* it? I find it easier to give in and just enjoy the way he possesses the parts of me I let him have.

I won't run. I haven't attempted to leave him since that night out in the rain. For so many reasons, it's easier to play the part of his passive captive, especially since he's given me a small taste of freedom.

Maybe before Carter, I would've bolted at my next chance. Not now.

Not *yet*.

Burns is still suspicious. Obviously, and I don't blame him. He hasn't threatened me with the cuffs again, and I'm not sure how he'll react when he goes back on the job when his vacation is over, but I'm learning things about him, too.

In his broken mind, he equates fucking me with keeping me. A ring with *forever*...

Since I'm sleeping in his bed instead of on the cot in the basement, Burns arrogantly believes I'm one kiss, one lick, one crooked grin away from finally giving in to him and staying with him in his hideaway.

I still refuse.

It's not even about sex anymore. Until I can be a

hundred percent sure that he won't use me and discard me like everyone else in my life has, I *can't* give in. What if it's all about possession with him? What if he gets what he wants, then decides the shine on me has worn off and I'm tossed aside?

I spent five years looking over my shoulder for Carter Santorino and rotten fuckers just like him. Could I return to my old life, simply waiting for the moment someone blames me for his death?

Would Burns even *let* me?

He thinks fucking me will make me want to stay. I'm terrified that fucking him will effectively end this little game we're playing. Right now, sex with Burns is the last thing—the *only* thing—I can hold over him. As much as my body aches to be dominated by his, I can't give it to him.

I don't know how much longer I'll be able to hold out. At first, it was because I refused to let my captor have everything he wanted. But after Carter... it's hard to understand, but what has started as obsession and captivity and *sex* has turned into something different.

Something *more.*

I would've never thought it'd be possible when I first woke up in the basement, but Burns and me... we've actually developed a homey routine. I can go hours at a time without thinking about my old life in Springfield. Escape? Sometimes I wonder what I'd even be escaping *to.*

Would it be worth it?

Returning to a dead-end job? My crummy apartment?

Last night, Burns mentioned getting me a computer. I'll never want to go back to a college campus. We both know that, even though the reason why is buried somewhere behind Burns's cabin. Still, I made it through three years of FU before I dropped out. I have credits. I could actually get my degree by doing online school.

That's not all, either. As one last 'fuck you' to Carter, Burns promised me that, in the spring, I can start my own garden in the backyard. I can plant any flower I want—including kiftsgate roses—and use Carter's corpse to nourish them.

I cheekily tell him that I'll want hundreds of daisies out back before realizing what I've done.

It's October. I don't know the exact date, but spring? That's like six months away—and I basically committed to sticking around until then.

Now he's standing in front of me, a crooked grin on his wickedly handsome face as he tells me to hurry up and shower. That we have reservations in an hour.

Of course, because he needs to get ready, too, we share the shower. I have to remind him of these so-called 'reservations' once or twice when he decides he'd rather to lick my pussy clean instead of just using a washcloth, but we're both dressed with ten minutes to spare.

I honestly thought it was a gag. That Burns set up dinner in the kitchen in a bid to finally get me to wear that sexy red dress he picked out for me.

I was *wrong*.

About a five-minute drive from his secluded cabin, there's a small town. He doesn't give me the name, though he says the population is less than five hundred. It's a hamlet. A place where everyone knows everyone's name—and their business, too. It boasts a single inn, two rival restaurants, a post office, and... that's really about it.

One restaurant does a decent Italian, he tells me. The other is standard American fare with burgers and fries. Considering he's dashing as all hell in a black button-down shirt, matching slacks, and his polished shoes, I figure he chose Italian.

I'm right about that.

As he parks the truck in front of the restaurant, I can't help but squint over at him.

Recently, Burns's whole attitude has become much more relaxed. Almost like his being my captor has taken a toll on him, and he only started to show me his more sensitive side after I stopped fighting him so much.

I'm enjoying getting to know this new Burns. The idea of going out to eat with him had intrigued me when he took my hand in his, leading me to the truck before helping me up into the cab.

Now? I'm not so sure.

I fiddle with the sleek skirt of the red dress before blurting out, "Is this another test?"

"I wouldn't say that." At my disbelieving look, Burns adds, "I've got a good reputation up in the hills. Even if you told any of these people that I brought you to my cabin and chained you up there, they'd never believe you. I know it hurts you when people don't, so I wouldn't even bother if I were you."

Okay. That wasn't the answer I was expecting. It was brutal and honest, just like the Burns I've come to know, but there was also a hint of... *protectiveness* weaved into his suddenly cavalier tone.

My hands land in my lap. "I... you really care if I'm hurt?"

He was cavalier in his earlier response—but not so much in his next one.

Leaning toward me, laying his hand on my exposed thigh, he gives it a gentle squeeze. "More than anything, angel."

Damn it.

I wish I didn't believe him. It would be so much easier to continue to hate Burns if he wanted to use me the same way that Carter did. And though he's been open from the beginning that he won't be satisfied until he owns every part of me from the inside out, he's held true to his word. He even made up for how close he came to being just like Carter.

Despite the tears suddenly stinging my eyes, looking back, I realize that while both men were dangerous to my health, only one ever cared that he is.

This one.

Mason Burns is a madman with a sense of honor. No conscience, but he won't lie to me no matter how many times I do it to him.

Now, just because he doesn't lie to me, that doesn't mean he's honest to a fault. Or maybe he is, but he's part delusional, too.

And I see evidence of that once we leave the truck and Burns leads me inside of the restaurant. It smells of garlic and oregano in here, with a dated vibe that works for the place, but something's off. After the hostess seats us at a cozy table at the back of the small restaurant, I realize what it is that's bothering me: everyone inside is watching us.

The Italian restaurant isn't completely full—there are maybe twelve other diners in here—but me and Burns... we have their complete attention.

I find out why a moment later when our waitress approaches our tale.

She's about Burns's age, maybe a year or two older. Pretty. Her strawberry-blonde hair is done up in a chic twist, complementing the simple black-and-white uniforms that all the servers seem to be wearing.

She gives him a warm smile. My gut goes tight with unexpected jealousy.

Crap. Why is she smiling at him?

"Hey, Mace. I've been seeing your truck around the hills a lot lately, but you haven't come to visit us for dinner. It's about time. How've you been?"

Mace.

Why is she calling him 'Mace'?

Yeah. It's his name. More than once, he's corrected me when I called him 'Burns', as though he'd prefer that I be as familiar with him as this waitress is.

Burns smiles back. I have to fist my hand in my lap to resist the urge to go for the butter knife next to the complimentary bread on the table.

Wait a sec—

I know that smile. It's the fake, friendly one I've seen him flash a hundred times before. The deceptively charming one that fooled me in the beginning.

It's not the secret, crooked grin that he shares with me.

Maybe... maybe there's no reason to be jealous, Ang. Remember what he said. No one has to know about us. I'm his dirty little secret, right?

That might be all I am—

"Good to see you, too, Stephanie. Job keeps me busy, you know, but it's always nice to come up for a hunt." He slides a teasing look my way. "It's my favorite pastime."

I can't tell if he's referring to me, or to Carter. Either way, I stay quiet.

No one has to know...

"I'm glad. What about your friend? I don't think we've had the pleasure of meeting before."

"That's because I've been hiding her."

Stephanie laughs. Burns chuckles.

I sit there like a freaking deer in headlights.

He just... he just admitted the truth. And he was right. She wouldn't believe a word of what happened to me if I opened my trap up and actually told her.

He has her fooled. He probably has them all fooled.

And I start to wonder: am I fooled, too? Or am I the only one who sees Mason Burns for who he truly is?

I don't get too long to think about that. Because, on the heels of that truth, he tells one hell of a lie. Worse, I'm absolutely sure he believes he's still being honest.

"Stephanie, this is Angela Havers. My fiancée. So you'll be seeing a lot more of her around."

"Fiancée?" Her deep brown eyes light up. I decide I won't hate her on principle if only because she actually looks pleased at Burns's complete fabrication instead of envious. "Congratulations, Mace. Hear that, everyone? Mace is getting hitched!"

At her announcement, it seems like the entire damn room cheers out loud, calling their congratulations to us.

"Dinner's on us," beams Stephanie, pulling out her waitress pad. "Whatever you want, we'll get it right out for you two."

Wearing a grin that can only be described as shit-eating, Burns places our orders for us. Ravioli for me, eggplant parm for him, and a bottle of red to split. I know it's his way of, once again, recreating that fateful date I had with Dean.

I couldn't care less right now.

I'm a little bit more preoccupied with how he just told an entire fucking restaurant that his captive is his future bride.

My mom was one thing. That was such a stereo-typically 'Burns' thing to do. Then again, I guess, so is this.

He'd knocked me speechless from the moment he led me into the restaurant, his hand clutching mine, my half-dressed body nestled against his side.

Finally, once the waitress bustles away, I find my voice again.

"I thought no one has to know," I toss at him under my breath.

In response to my comment, Burns rises partway out of his seat. Before I realize what he's about to do, he leans over the table, hand outstretched.

I asked him for a hairbrush and a blow dryer the other day and he got them for me; the fact that the cabin didn't have either until I requested them of my captor just proved to me that he wasn't full of shit when he said I was the only woman to stay there. Time was short after our shower and the most I managed to do was let my hair fall in soft waves down my back before we had to go.

With the entire restaurant as witness, Burns threads his fingers through my hair. Once he's palmed the back of my head, he tilts it away from him. On a surprised gasp, my lips part. He kisses me to a few smattering rounds of applause.

Breathless, I'm staring up at him as he releases his hold on my head. His steely blue eyes are twinkling in the candlelight as he licks his lip, then grins as he says, "I *lied*."

Huh. I guess there's a first time for everything.

EIGHTEEN
MASON

ANGELA

Burns isn't just his name, I've decided. It's what he does to me.

One touch and I'm on fire, even though I know that this—*us*—is so wrong. Even if he swears that I'll love him one day, and not just how he controls me.

He's determined to wait, and since he has me trapped in his cabin with no escape, there's nothing I can do but wait with him—and hope that his unshakable obsession with me really is his way of showing me his love.

He stalked me. Watched me. Even broke into my bedroom to learn more about me.

He thought he could use it to break me, to make me his.

Maybe he could have. If I was the old Angela... I don't know if I would've made it past my first night in his cabin. But I'm not the old Angela anymore, and knowing that Burns is obsessed with me... that he *chose* me... is fulfilling every secret kink I have never admitted out loud before.

I can trace it back to the night we killed Carter; because, despite who fired the fatal shot, we both had a hand in taking out the bogeyman from my nightmares. I doubt I'll ever tell another soul, but the way he *murdered* for me?

It was inevitable. *We* were inevitable.

I always thought that one of us would break first.

Turns out, it was *me*.

OKAY. SO, FIRST OF ALL, WHAT HAPPENED AFTER DINNER?

It wasn't what I set out to do. Not really.

Well, not *intentionally*...

I would even love to say it was the single glass of red wine I had with dinner that went to my head, but that would be a fucking lie, too.

I knew what I was doing. When I asked Burns to unzip me, then walked around the bedroom in only my panties and my bra, I knew how his body would react.

When I—whoops—unsnapped my bra, and stepped out of the panties, I almost expected him to whip out his dick and start jerking off right in front of me. He's done it before. He told me so, when he admitted that he would masturbate while I slept.

Thankfully, he cleaned up any of his mess before he snuck back out of my place. I'd also be lying if I said it didn't get me fucking hot to know that my sleeping body could get such a rise out of him.

My naked body does, too.

Was I teasing him? Later, I'll admit that I was. For all his big talk about owning my pussy and wanting to fuck my hair wild, he hasn't made another move since I started sleeping in his bed. Up until dinner, I began to wonder if he somehow lost his attraction to me. Showing off my naked body was a surefire way to make sure he didn't.

And, boy, does it work.

I'm naked. Burns has pulled off his shirt and his shoes, sitting there in only his unzipped jeans. His hand rests lightly on his cock, highlighting the erection he isn't even trying to hide.

"You keep walking around like that, I can't be responsible for what I do to you."

I give him a mischievous grin. "You said you'd never force me."

He wipes his mouth with the back of his hand. "Did say that, didn't I?"

"You said you'd wait for me to beg you to fuck me if you had to."

He gulps. "Sounds like me."

I lean in, making sure my tits brush against his bare chest. "You said you'd fuck my hair wild."

"Angel... you're playing with fire. You know that, right?"

"No," I say earnestly, grabbing his cock. "I'm playing with Burns. Only I'm not playing." I squeeze. "I'm begging."

So, yeah. I know exactly what I was doing. Because after that? There was no going back.

One second, I've got my hand on his cock. The next? His pants are going flying, his big body pushing mine back against the bed.

"Once I get inside of you, forget any ideas of ever escaping me. You're mine. You'll always be mine. Understand?"

He says that like I have a choice. With him, there isn't any.

I don't think there ever was.

Inevitable...

For over a week he's told me that I want him. Right now, panting beneath him, his weight comforting me in a way that surprises me, I *do*.

But I have to ask first. "Aren't you going to grab a condom?"

I might have accepted that sex with my captor—with Burns—has always been inevitable, that though I haven't quite given up on the idea that I could return to my old life one day, I wasn't walking away without finding out what it would be like to be utterly possessed by Mason Burns if only just once... but I've never slept with anyone without a condom before. It's a level of trust, vulnerability, and intimacy I've never had with another soul.

I should've known better. When Burns says he owns me, he means it.

"You're going to take every drop of my come like a good girl with nothing between us. You understand me, angel? Now say 'yes, officer'."

I have half a mind to kick him in the ass and shove him off of me. But the other half... the deranged, perverted half that's fantasized over this moment far more than it ever should have... takes control as I murmur throatily, "Yes, officer."

He told me I would beg. He told me that, no matter what, he wasn't going to stop until he got to fuck me.

What he didn't tell me? Was that all it would take is a simple 'yes'.

The second I say it, he grips his cock by the base and presses it to the entrance of my pussy. I'm so wet, he slides a little, but Burns is nothing if not determined. He readjusts himself, shoving with enough force to get the first couple of inches inside of me before I let out a soft coo.

"You doing okay, angel?"

I haven't been fucked in more than five years. Burns's fingers might have stretched me a little when he fingerfucked me, but two fingers versus his thick dick? Yeah... it takes me a second to get used to the intrusion.

"If you'd rather wait... or foreplay. Let me give you head—"

"No." He's already lodged inside of me. "Keep going. I... I can take it."

He doesn't look so sure. Then again, there's no denying he wants this terribly. Unless I tell him to 'stop', he's not going to.

He gave me a chance. He gave me an out. When I refuse it, he says, "Hold tight," and, next thing I know, he's more than halfway in.

"Ah, shit... I... okay. I'm good. You can... keep going."

"For you, angel, anything."

One last shove and I really hope that's everything he has because I can't take another inch.

You know what, though? It feels fucking *fabulous*.

My hands fly up on their own accord. One hand goes to his gorgeous chest, stroking his peck. The other lands on his forearm, swiping the daisy tattoo with his thumb.

"Oh, Burns…"

MACE

"Oh, Burns…"

Burns.

My head is half-clouded with the promise of pleasure. My balls have gone tight. The last time I got laid, it was three years ago, I had an itch, and it meant nothing. I hadn't had the desire to get off with another soul since—until my angel shyly handed me a daisy, and I went hard as a fucking rock when her delicate little hand brushed against mine.

I never thought I'd get a chance to work my cock inside of her. Back then, she was too pure, and I was too tainted. I would ruin her for a night of pleasure and, proving that I'm not a completely selfish bastard, I tried to stay away.

Tried.

Failed.

Between my near-daily patrols and how damn often I slipped into her unlocked window, the only thing I didn't do was touch her. I fantasized about doing that all the fucking time, rubbing one out to her gentle smile, her haunted eyes, and her soft touch.

When she finally wrapped her hand around my

cock, I thought it couldn't get any better. Then I worked my entire length into her welcoming sheath and, holy fuck, I was wrong.

With my angel pinned on my cock, that pretty, pretty hair splayed on my pillow like I've always wanted, I know that there's only one thing in this world that would make this the best fucking night of my life.

Angela's complete surrender.

Burns...

She's always called me that. Until now, it didn't really bother me. Most people do, and those who don't, stick with 'Mace'.

Not her. I need my angel to be different.

I need her to be mine, yes, but more than anything, I need to be *hers.*

So, once I've bottomed out inside of her, I hold. As she explores my body, whispering my surname, I refuse to move. A shiver skitters down my back, every instinct inside of my body urging me to thrust, to move, to *claim,* but this is the first time I've finally shown her just how much I possess her.

It's her turn to own me. To claim me.

To show me that everything I've done has been worth it.

Dipping low, I steal a fierce kiss that leaves her lush lips pouty and bruised. My arms are locked, my body still, and when I draw away, my pretty little angel squirms beneath me like a moth pinned to a board. Stuffed full of my cock, she wants me to move as much as I do.

But first—

"Not Burns," I tell her. My voice is hoarse. The strain is evident in the way I spit out my command. "When I'm inside of you, you call me by my name. You call me Mason."

When she doesn't answer me quick enough, I slowly pull out, making sure she feels it in every damn one of her nerve endings.

I'm punishing myself more than her—I just got my cock wet, damn it—but this is important to me. I could order her, and she would obey. I could stroke myself off right now, finishing on her stomach, marking her again... that would soothe the need raging inside of me.

But it's more than that. I don't want her to fuck Burns. I want her to open herself up to Mason.

My chest is heaving. She's spread out beneath me, one arm stretched over her head as though she's still cuffed to one of my headboards. The fingers on her other hand dig into the sheets, flexing and clutching as her tits rise and fall.

My mark on her skin trembles. The letters seem to shake, only that's her.

Angela's breath is as frantic as mine, her pebbled

nipples brushing against my skin as I bend my elbows just enough to close the gap between us.

She gasps. But she still doesn't say my fucking name.

Leaning on my left arm, putting all of my weight on it, I grab my cock by the base of it, positioning the head right where it belongs. She's so fucking hot, so *wet*, I slide right past the opening to her pussy. The head bumps against her clit, and while she shudders out a breath, I swallow my moan.

I wedge my hips between hers, forcing them wider. She squirms, but even if I was inclined to let her get away, I can tell that her heart's not in it. My angel doesn't want to give in that easily, but we both know she will. That's what makes her such a good girl. She's begged for my fingers and writhed while I buried my face in her pussy, she's stroked me off, sucked my cock, and she even let me shove my cock all the way inside of her... she'll give me this, too.

I'll demand it.

Dipping my head, keeping my hot cock pressed against her lower belly, I lap at the tattoo I inked on her what seems like a lifetime ago. To me, it is. My forever didn't start until the moment I had my angel here with me, and I'm looking forward to every day that will follow.

But first—

I rock against her as I nuzzle her tit, paying special

attention to the tattoo there. As her breathing picks up, combined with a keening whine, I go a little lower. Sucking her nipple in my mouth, I suck, I lick, I even bite... and, still, she stubbornly refuses to give me what I want.

She's tilting her hips, though, desperate for some relief. I hide my smile against her nipple as Angela arches her back, trying to guide me back inside of her.

Not yet, angel. Not until I get what I desire.

"Who do you want to fuck you?"

She's still trying to entice the head of my cock inside of her. But she isn't using my name.

I could slip it back in so easily. I won't. I need this concession from her more than I need to come.

"Tell me, angel. Who do you want to fuck you?"

She grunts. I've never thought a grunt could be so fucking sexy until Angela does it.

That almost breaks me. I want to fuck her so bad. I want to fill her up with my come like I told her I would. I've had my way so many times with her, maybe this once I could let her win.

I pull back, shifting my hips so that I'm pressed right against her heat.

I'm not teasing anymore. I want this from her, but if we're going to be a union, there's gotta be some compromise, right?

"Damn it! Mason, okay? I want you to fuck me, Mason."

Oh. Well.

I lift my head, making sure she sees my smile this time. "Whatever you want, angel," then push all the way back inside of her.

The teasing didn't help either of us. Within my first few strokes, Angela is clutching my hips, guiding me into her. She wants it hard, promising me she can take it, and I'm too driven by lust to double-check. Just like I thought, hearing her say my full name drove me wild. In my fevered brain, she was admitting what I've known all along.

That we were meant for each other.

I'll fuck her. I'll breed her, too, if that's what it takes to keep her. When I fill her up with my come, I'll know that I've reached parts of her no one else has.

Condom? I warned her before. No one can come between us.

Nothing can come between us.

We're one. We always will be.

And as she throws back her head, her pussy squeezing me so tightly, it's impossible for me to keep from coming inside of her, the fact that she remembers to moan my name has my semi fucking the creampie I gave her.

"Every drop, angel," I say raggedly. If I have to use my cock to shove it as far as I go, I will. "Such a good girl. Every inch and every drop."

With dazed hazel eyes locked on me, she nods,

then throws her hands over my shoulders, hanging on for the ride while I leisurely stroke inside of her.

"Yes, Mason..."

I shudder at the way she murmurs my name.

Finally—*finally*—I've made my angel mine. Nothing will ever come between us again.

No matter what I have to do, I'll make sure of it— and not even Angela herself will be able to stop me.

NINETEEN
ANGELA'S BOOK

MACE

I wait to see if she'll regret it. To turn my claiming of her into another transaction. A way for her to justify her actions while blaming me for them.

When she doesn't, I smile.

It's an honest grin. The one I save only for her.

From that moment on, she's mine.

The best part is, she always *was*.

It took a lot of time to get here. Scheming. Manipulating. I don't regret a second of it, or a single thing I did to make sure that Angela wanted me as much as I craved her. From the daisy to the date, it was only a matter of taking any advantage I could.

I always knew that, with the right tool, I'd be able to keep her forever.

My angel... she was born to run. Never staying in one place for long, always looking over her shoulder. All she's ever wanted was someone to love her. To cherish her. To choose her above all, and provide her with the security she's chased her whole adult life.

She wanted *me*.

I thought my obsession was too dark for her. I thought that I was no good. My angel deserved a good man, not a possessive bastard who rifled through her belongings when she was asleep—or who betrayed her by reading her journal the moment he got his hands on it.

I don't regret that, either. Without the journal, I would've continued to keep my distance. Always watching, forever lusting, but I would never have corrupted her.

Not unless she *wanted* to be corrupted.

And Angela... she did. More than that, she wanted Officer Burns to do the corrupting.

I was happy to oblige.

Once I realized exactly what a goldmine her private journal was, any idea that I would let my angel live her sweet little life without me went up in flames. Flipping through the pages whenever I got the chance, I followed it like it was a fucking guidebook. Even after I loaded her in my cruiser, I made sure to grab the journal.

I had to reassure myself that what I was doing was right. That it was what she wanted.

When I watched her struggle to be my prisoner, the journal reinforced my plan. When I inadvertently made her cry, I read the passages about what that fucker Santorino did to her again and realized my mistake. Pleasuring her was easy. Letting her give herself permission to touch me wasn't.

But that's because she didn't want permission. She wanted me to take, so I did.

Everything she wanted. Everything she desired. Everything my sweet, broken angel, my pretty little florist kept hidden in the dark recesses of her cracked heart... to make it whole—to make it *mine*—I did it all.

Now I have her body. In the week following the first time she let me fuck her, all I have to do is grin and she's ready and willing for me. I won't stop until she has my ring on her finger; then I'll have her soul. Loyalty will come in time.

But I still don't have her heart.

I'm going back on duty tomorrow. The two weeks have been a whirlwind, and if I thought that giving up the job would make Angela happy, I'd quit tonight. She likes knowing I'm a cop. That's one of the things that attracted me to her in the first place and I'd be a fucking moron if I gave that up until I had my wife completely locked down.

The idea of leaving her behind doesn't sit right with me. I can't bring myself to put her back in the basement, but I know I'll live up to my name and burn the whole fucking world down if she gave me her body, then tried to run. I want to believe that I did enough to convince her that I'm the best man for her.

I want to, but my angel is a complicated woman.

Thank fucking God for the journal.

As much as I'd prefer spending every second until I have to go back on patrol with Angela, I sneak away the night before. I've been trying to show her that I stopped thinking of her as my prisoner—not that I truly ever did—and she's taken well to having free rein of the whole cabin.

I left her in the living room, tucked beneath a blanket, watching some kind of Halloween special. After kissing her and promising I'd be back before the next ad, I slipped away to the bedroom.

There's got to be something I missed in her journal. Something that can help me figure out what move to make next to keep Angela dangling on my hook. I like to keep her on her toes. If she stops and thinks too long, she might realize she can do so much better than me.

She can. I refuse to let her.

I've read this journal cover to cover at least ten times. It spans the entire time she lived in Springfield, and I've marked the pages when she mentions me in particular. The rest is just noise. My temper gets too hot to handle when I read about other guys or the shit hand she'd been dealt. It's only ever been about me and her.

I have to keep it that way.

"Come on," I mutter under my breath, going from page to page. "Come on—"

"Burns?"

Fuck. My head jerks up, dropping the journal in my lap. It's too late. She already saw what I had.

My angel is a fucking goddess. Standing there, tousled hair hanging over her shoulders, my tattoo a dark brand on her creamy skin, I love seeing her in the flesh. It's my favorite fucking sight in the world.

But not when she loses all color as she stares at the book I dropped.

"Where... where did you get that?"

Fuck!

ANGELA

I'm naked.

These last few days, with Burns's desire to spend as much time inside of me as he can, and my willingness to let him... I haven't seen a reason to get dressed. When I didn't want to distract him with my pussy or my tits, I grabbed his SPD shirt—well, *my* SPD shirt now—and tugged it on, knowing it was only a matter of time before I was yanking it off again.

Burns loves playing with my boobs during sex, but that's nothing compared to his masculine pride when he sees the healed tattoo of his name and badge number branded on my chest.

But though I'm completely bare right now, I've never felt more vulnerable in my life than when I walked into the bedroom and saw Burns rifling through my journal.

My *journal*.

It was the therapist I saw after my assault who suggested I work through my emotions by journaling. In writing down how I was feeling, I might find some kind of peace. The opposite happened. The things I wrote down... the secret thoughts I admitted because no one else was supposed to know them... I realized just how broken I am.

How broken I think I've always been.

And Burns *knows*.

I hold out my hand. I can stop this. I can pretend it's not happening. If only I can get that book away from him...

"Give it to me."

"Angela—"

"Give it to me!"

"Angel, baby... let's talk about this."

"You said you didn't read it! You lied to me!"

The look he gives me, I know what he's going to say even before he does.

"I never said I didn't. But if you want to talk about who's been lying to who all along..." Burns raps the cover of my journal with his knuckles. "I've got a few passages earmarked."

"Burns, don't—"

"I told you from the beginning, angel. Sometimes you have to be prepared to be disappointed. And before you ask, this isn't a punishment. It's not a reward, either. It's about coming clean." His gaze locks on mine. Any other time I've been naked around him, he never hid how much he ogled me. Now? He's staring right into my eyes.

I'd rather he be talking to my tits.

I swallow roughly. "What if I begged?"

His lips quirk. "You'd only like it."

Oh, God. He did it. He really read it. He's not bluffing.

And the bastard wasn't lying. I can see dog-eared pages, as though he's returned to them repeatedly.

Clearing his throat, he opens my journal and begins to read one out loud.

"'I gave Officer Burns a daisy today. I don't know what came over me. I just... I wanted him to notice me.'" Glancing up from the page, his expression softens. "Oh, angel. Believe me, I already noticed... but the second you gave me the daisy, you sealed your fate. I knew you were meant to be mine."

That's why I did it. Why I purposely sought him out and handed him the flower. I never thought he would care—and, yeah, I was wrong about that one—but, all along, back when he was just Officer Burns, I was dying for him to notice me.

He was so strong. So kind. Fucking gorgeous. Nothing like the cops in Fairview who ridiculed me. Who made me feel like I was worthless. His smile could brighten my whole day, and I started to believe that such a good cop like Officer Burns would help me when no one else ever has.

Isn't that twisted? The cops failed me, and I pinned all my hopes... all my affection... on a beat cop who walked by the shop where I worked.

So I gave him a daisy, and I smiled back, and then he saved me from Brick...

Ah, Brick. I kind of feel bad about that now. I honestly believed that, deep down, Burns was a good guy. Up until the moment he arrested me, I had a bit of fantasy about what he was like. I think part of me recognized the darkness in him—the same as what blossomed inside of me following what happened in Fairview—because my other fantasies...

I left my window open on purpose to tempt him. I accepted Dean's date for the same reason. Before that, I even gave Brick fifty bucks to pretend to rob me when

I knew that Burns was doing a nighttime patrol. All I wanted was for the good cop to save me, to *see* me.

And then Burns showed the world—and me—that he was following his own brand of justice. He killed him because Brick held me up with the knife I gave the poor kid to use.

Oops.

Maybe he shouldn't have accidentally nicked me with it, huh?

On the plus side, at least I never mentioned that part in my journal. I talked about how happy I was to prove that Burns was a hero. How he did what I thought he would, running after Brick and taking him down for the attack.

Of course, Brick had no idea that was my plan. Dumb kid just saw the dollar signs, not the aftermath. Then again, neither did I.

But just because I didn't jot that down, it doesn't mean there aren't hundreds of other secret confessions I never wanted Burns to read.

Like this one—

"'Sometimes I think about putting a secret mark on me. Like a flame... something that shows how much I want him to be mine without anyone else knowing. A tattoo just for us.'"

He glances up again. "You gave me the idea. I was always pretty handy with a tattoo gun, and I gave myself the daisy as a nod to what you wanted. Then, when I took you home with me, I put my name on you. You know why?"

I can't even speak. Stunned and horrified that he doesn't seem the least bit fazed by what he's reading, I shake my head.

"Because I want the whole fucking world to know you're mine. I'll give a flame if you want, but Burns... it's gonna be your name, too, angel. Might as well get used to it."

Angela Burns.

Angela *Burns*—

He's reading the journal again.

"'I want someone to protect me... to show me that I matter...' That's me. It'll always be me." He flicks ahead a few more pages. "'I just wish that fucker was dead. After what he did to me... the way he used me... I'd kill him if I could...' I gave you the chance. But, let me tell you, if you ever used his name instead of calling him 'fucker', he would've been dead the first time I had to read how he hurt you."

That's right. In every journal entry I ever wrote about Carter, I called him 'fucker' because, well, that's what he was. And I wanted him dead. God, did I wish I could be the one to do it.

Yet, when I missed, Burns did it for me.

My mouth falls open. The only thing I can think to say is, "Stop."

He glances over the top of the journal. "Do you

really want me to? Maybe we could talk about how you fantasized about me pulling my gun on you and making you go to your knees. That's in here. So's the idea that I bend you over in public. I like that one."

The rain was a nice touch. So was the trap that let me think I was close to getting away, even when I desperately wanted to stay...

"Yes. Stop. *Please.*"

This time, he slams the journal closed. "If that's what you want, baby."

That's not at all what I really want—and, damn it, he knows that, too.

I'm trembling. When Burns makes a move toward me, I hold up my hand. He immediately stills.

"How much?"

"How much what?"

I gulp. "How much of it... of us... was real?"

He understands immediately what I'm getting at.

"Every fucking minute of it."

I wish I could believe that.

When I turn away from him, not even holding my hand up, warding him off, can keep him on the other side of the room. Dashing toward me, he takes both of mine in his. "Look at me, Angela."

I can't. I'm not sure what I'll see if I do.

Loathing? Disgust? Or, worse, that teasing smile that says that everyone's a fool for falling for Burns's facade?

Who is he? The man I imagined, the man I've spent weeks with, or someone else entirely?

"Look at me!"

Desperation fills his voice. For that reason alone, I dare a peek back at him.

Relief fills his gaze as he demands, "How did I find your journal?"

I don't know. I shrug.

"Answer me." When I glance away again, he lets go of my hands and grips my shoulders, forcing me to look up at him. "If I wasn't already in your room, how would I have found it? If I wasn't already obsessed, sneaking up the fire escape to watch you sleep, wishing you weren't too good... too much of an angel for a man like me... why would I do this?"

"I don't know."

"I did this for you. I gave you what you wanted because I love you, and if this is the man you want as yours, I'll be it. I'll be whatever the fuck you want because you're not going anywhere. Neither am I. We're it. You understand me?"

"I want to..."

"It's only ever been about what you wanted. Believe me." He tucks me against him, resting his chin on the top of my head. "Look, we're both broken. I was born this way. You were made this way. But that's the beauty of us, angel. No matter what, we can make each other whole. Forever has been built on less, and we have our mutual obsession and a taste for justice to keep us together."

"And blood," I whisper.

"Sometimes that's the same thing."

He isn't wrong.

"I want to understand, Burns... I do. Are you telling me that you did this? Taking me captive, making me scared... making me believe that, at any moment, you might become obsessed with someone else... you did this all for me?"

"Love can fade. I love you desperately, but sometimes that's not enough. But obsession? You're all I think about it. I close my eyes, I see your face. I lick my lips, I taste you. If I thought you'd let me, I'd fucking chain you to my side so that I would never have a heartbeat when I wasn't experiencing *you*."

He sounds so brutally honest, so achingly vulnerable, my only reaction is to break out of his hold.

Burns lets out a pained sound. "You weren't ready for the truth. Fuck. I did it again. I pushed you too far—"

"You didn't."

"Don't be scared of me," he pleads. "Not you, angel. Never you."

How can I be?

Maybe I *am* his angel, but he's my devil.

More than that, he's *mine*.

And now that I don't have to hide who I am anymore, it's time I prove it.

Right now, our roles are reversed. The parts we've played... we've swapped them. Burns is begging?

Okay. Then I'll take control.

"*Strip*."

TWENTY

THE TRUE STORY

ANGELA

He blinks. "What did you say?"

"Did I fucking stutter?" My voice comes out stronger than I've ever heard it. I sound cold, too, almost like I'm mimicking Burns. I *like* it. "Take your damn clothes off."

I don't have to tell him a third time. Within seconds, every last stitch of clothing is gone, Burns tossing it to the floor with the discarded journal until he's as naked as I am.

Laying my hand in the center of his chest, I give him a gentle shove, pushing him back on the bed until he's seated. I know I'm only able to move him because he's allowing me to do so. Good. He has no reason to try and stop me.

In fact, he seems utterly stunned—absolutely fucking *amazed*—as I curve my hand around his semi. It's no surprise that his cock is twitching a little from just the sight of me naked, and as I tug on his shaft, alternating between stroking him off and rubbing my thumb over the head of his dick, I make it my mission to get him hard as soon as possible.

Dropping down to a crouch, pressing kisses to his heated flesh, dabbing my tongue at the tip so I can catch any of the pre-come that beads there as I ready him for me... he's completely erect in no time.

Burns braces his hands on the mattress behind him, fisting the comforter as he lifts his hips, trying to push his hard-on past my lips so that I'll start sucking.

Uh-uh. Maybe later, but for now? I have something else in mind—and I'm pretty sure he's going to like that.

I slap his bobbing cock lightly, shoving him away from my face.

He hisses. "*Angel...*"

Rising up from my crouch, I grin. "Lean back, baby, and get comfortable."

He arches his eyebrows, but doesn't refuse. Instead, he scoots his naked ass backward until his back is up against the pillows cushioning the headboard. Then, with a daring smirk tugging on his lips, he folds his hands behind his head, waiting to see what I'm going to do next.

Once he's where I want him, I dip my hand between my legs, running my pointer finger up my slit. I'm already soaked, my fingertip slipping right through the moisture gathered there. Dropping all pretenses, showing Burns the real me... I've never been so fucking turned on.

I could draw this out. I could make him wait a little longer... but if I did that, I'd only be torturing myself.

I want him.

I can have him.

I'm going to *take* him.

And that's why I climb up on top of the bed. With his attention entirely on me, I swing one leg over both of his so that I'm straddling him. Making sure to face him—determined to watch every hint of his expression as I take control—I don't hesitate to guide his cock into me. Once I'm fully seated, his girth stretching me out deliciously, I pause only a moment to get used to him and then begin to *ride*.

One swivel of my hips and any amusement he'd been portraying disappears as hunger, as *need*, as want overtakes his features. Throwing back his head, he drops his hands to the bed as I work my body, racing my way toward completion.

Not my own, though. Oh, no. I need this man to come inside of me more than I need to breathe my next breath. I need to be his, for him to claim me the same time as I'm claiming him, to show him that we've always been meant to be.

So, yeah. I'm not chasing my own orgasm. This moment in time? This fuck that will change *everything*?

It's all about Mason Burns.

The lure of my bouncing breasts becomes too much for him. No longer clutching the comforter again, he reaches up, grabbing onto my tits. The heat of his palms sends shivers coursing down my spine, ripping a moan from me. But I love it, and I arch my back, making it easier for him to touch me.

He groans, eyes darkening as he meets mine. "That's it. I'm dreaming. No way... tell me this is all a dream because no fucking way this is real."

Up, down, up, down. I rise up, then let my full weight settle on him again and again, so focused on pleasuring my cop that I can barely answer him with my body. Words? Impossible.

Besides, if this is a dream, it belongs to me—just like this magnificent male does.

I completely own Mason Burns, his body—his heart, his *soul,* too—forever mine to do whatever I want with.

And I've been waiting a long fucking time for this.

"I thought you'd hate me," he says next, panting as he starts to move himself. I knew he wouldn't be able to let me keep total control the whole time, and he's shifting his hips, rising up desperately, frantic to match the pace I've set for us. "For everything I did to you... my biggest fear was that you'd wake up one morning and your feelings for me would be gone. That you'd believe I did everything I did for me, and not for you. That's why... oh, angel... I had to tell you that you wanted it. I didn't know what I would do if you ever stopped."

"Oh, baby," I tell him in a throaty voice, "I'll never stop."

One hand drops down again, reaching behind me so that he can grab my ass. He digs his fingers into the cheek, squeezing me tightly. "Promise me. Fucking *swear* it."

I can do better than that.

He squeezed my ass. Clenching my core, I squeeze my pussy around his cock as I command, "Come for me, Mason."

He gets such a thrill when I use his first name. Since I've trained him that I'll only call him 'Mason' when he's inside of me, he obviously equates it with fucking—and with coming. Sometimes just whispering his name is enough to edge him closer. Commanding it like that, like I'm his superior officer? That should've been enough to have him bucking up inside of me, releasing with a possessive roar.

But this is Burns. With a smirk and a need to also control me, sometimes he holds on just a little longer so that the sex lasts and he can remind me that he owns me, too.

Another squeeze as his lips curve in a dare. "You first, angel."

Uh-uh. Not this time, baby.

Tossing my hair back, bracing my hands against his sweat-slicked chest for a little more leverage, I quicken my pace. I clench my inner muscles even harder, jabbing my nails into his pecs because—just like me—a whisper of pain always leads him to going off like a damn rocket.

He's stubborn, too. If there's one thing I can say about Burns, it's that he's always been a generous lover with me. From the beginning, he made it seem like his whole purpose in life was to get me off.

It's about time I return the favor.

Luckily for me, I've got a trick that he'll never expect.

Leaning down so that my body is bowed over him, my tits brushing against his chest, my lips pressed to his left ear, I whisper, "I love you, Mason."

"Fucking damn it," he grunts, wrapping his arms around me, pulling me flush against his chest as he finally does buck up into me. His movements are quick, shallow thrusts that come to a full stop as his body jerks, his orgasm slamming into him as he shoots his load inside of me.

Ha. Smiling into his chest, I think: *I win.*

Burns clutches me to him, rubbing his palms along the small of my back as he purposely keeps us connected.

Once he can speak again, he demands, "Tell me you meant it, angel. Tell me you love me."

I meant it the first time. When he held that gun to his head and life without Burns flashed before my eyes, I fucking meant it. I just didn't let him know that.

What kind of whacko falls for her cruel captor within days of being kidnapped? Who wants their first confession of love to be forced from them at gunpoint?

Who manipulated the whole situation so that would be the outcome?

Turns out the answer is *me*.

"Would I lie to you?" I tease, shifting my head so that my cheek is pressed to his chest. His heart is pounding wildly, and my grin widens.

That fucker beats for me—and I love knowing that almost as much as I love Mason Burns.

Of course, my glib answer isn't what Burns is hoping for. Probably not what he was expecting, either. But now I've finally discovered just how he got to know me as well as he did. It wasn't simply stalking me or watching over me from a distance. My journal is like a portal straight to my brain so he should've known better than to ever doubt my feelings for him.

After all, they're right there in black and white.

As I content myself, listening to his heartbeat

settle, Burns shifts his position just enough so that he can slip his fingers between our slick bodies. I know instinctively that he's going for my clit to make sure that I also come.

It's a sweet gesture, but not necessary. Later, he can make me come all he wants. Now that I've made sure he's finished, there's something else I want to do first. On the heels of both of us making our confessions, I can't see any reason to postpone it any longer —and I don't want to, either.

So, pushing up off of his chest, I shove until I'm sitting up on top of Burns, then move back so that his dick slides out of me. Another slap—to his fingers this time—and he gets the hint that I'm good for the moment. Though it's obvious from the shadows that flutter across his hollowed face that letting go of me is the last thing he wants to do, Burns will give me whatever the hell I want, including space when I need it.

As long as I don't go too far from him, that is. I don't plan on it. In this case, all I have to do is slip around the bed to where my lover left his pants after he kicked them off before.

When I bend over to reach for them, Burns lets out a pained groan that has me grinning to myself. Hurriedly, I pat his discarded pants, triumphant when I find the box-shaped bulge in one of his pockets. I yank it out, not even a little surprised that he's still carrying the ring box with him. When it's not on the dresser in our room, mocking me, it's in his possession.

Not for much longer.

I toss it at Burns.

My suave, cool, collected cop actually fumbles the catch. He does recover quickly, snapping the lid open, plucking the ring from the box.

He knows me. Better than myself, I think, but even if he didn't, it's obvious why I gave him the ring.

Because I want him to give it to *me*.

"Angela... if I put this on your finger, that's it. Nothing short of you stabbing me in the fucking heart will get me to agree to let you take it off again. Even then, I'll plead with you as I bleed out to keep it on until I'm dead and can't see you without it. I'm that fucking serious. Do you understand me?"

Perfectly.

He made me his personal prisoner. He cuffed me to a bed in his basement. He took his gun out and told me to get on my knees, keeping it in his hand the entire time I sucked his dick before admitting that it was empty.

He killed Carter for me, and he's proudly confessed that Carter isn't the only one.

He did everything to show me that he was a bad man—or, at least, that Burns saw himself that way—

Joining him on the bed again, rising up on my knees in front of him, I stick my hand out. As he readily shoves the wedding band on my ring finger, I can't help but chuckle because, well, it didn't work.

So maybe he is a bad man. He's still *mine*.

The golden band is a perfect fit. I twist my hand, watching the light play off of the metal.

"You told my mom I was your fiancée," I remind him. "Same with all those people in the restaurant. I wouldn't want to make a liar out of you, Burns."

"Mason," he reminds me.

Uh-uh. Not right now, he isn't.

Of course, that's easily remedied...

Wearing his ring, I inch closer to him, dropping my hand to the base of his shaft. Even though I've already milked him, his cock is back to semi-hard.

Eh. That's good enough for me.

Throwing my leg over his lap once more, I use my left hand to grab his cock—already thickening, as though expecting what's going to come next—and insert him back into my slick pussy. Then, once he's as firmly lodged inside as he can be, I drop all the way down again, connecting our bodies completely so that he can't slip out.

I wrap my hands around his neck, my thumbs pointing at the hollow of his throat. Why not? Every time he's done that to me, I found it a struggle not to cream my panties then and there.

I always thought it was because I was broken. Nope. I just required an obsessed male who understands what I want—and knows how to give me just what I need.

I need...

"Mason," I purr.

Grabbing my ass, tucking me against him again, he rolls until I'm flat on my back beneath him. As I squeal in delight, not sure if I enjoy his show of strength more or the way he's thrusting into me already, he dips his head.

Good thing my tattoo is completely healed otherwise it would've hurt like fucking hell when he digs his teeth into the mark he branded on my skin.

He doesn't hurt me. The opposite really.

It feels fucking *amazing*.

Burns lathes his bite mark with his tongue, paying special attention to my tattoo. I know why. Not only was it his way of fulfilling one of my deepest, darkest fantasies, but it's physical proof that I'm his.

I could take the ring off as easily as he slid it on. But the ink. *Never*.

It's the ultimate sign that I belong to Mason Burns.

Just like I've always wanted...

As I lay back, taking the pounding as he fucks me deeper and deeper, giving me some pleasure of my own as he dominates me, I caress his neck, then bury my fingers in his sweat-dampened dark hair. A bit of a wicked tease comes over me again as he mutters my name, grinding his groin against mine.

"Mason, baby?"

He grunts, fingers on my hip, pinning me in place so that he can rock into me madly, barely slowing his pace as he answers me. "Yes, angel?"

"So.. about our true love story—"

Mason's grin turns devilish. "You mean how I obsessed over you for months, snuck into your apartment to watch you sleep, eventually read your journal, discovered to my fucking delight that you were just as obsessed with me so I went on to fulfill every single one of your very *descriptive* fantasies to make you mine forever?"

Very succinct summary there, babe, and all without missing a stroke.

Hey. It's not like I can deny it, either. The evidence is all in the journal he stole from my bedroom.

"That's right."

He parts his lips. Taking the invitation for what it is, I lift my head and kiss him with all the passion that I forced myself to hide. When I finally had gotten what I wanted—his attention—I didn't want to scare him off so soon.

I wanted to be his angel—and I *am*.

Breaking the kiss, he rests his forehead against mine, still moving his hips with a determination to make me take every inch of him until I forget anyone that had ever come before him.

Mason huffs out a breath, murmuring softly, "It'll be our dirty little secret."

See? He knows exactly what kind of woman I am—just like I adore the kind of guy my cop is.

Mine.

"You were right all along, Mason," I whisper against his lips. He's still inside of me, and I hope he never leaves. "No one has to know."

MACE
POLICE

NO ONE HAS TO KNOW

ANGELA
FLORIST

AUTHOR'S NOTE

Thanks for reading *No One Has To Know*!

While this is a standalone, I'm excited to say that this isn't the last time you'll see Angela and Burns. They have a cameo in the main series that is set in the seedier side of Springfield, showing up in the first book that features the infamous Devil that Burns mentioned in his POV: *The Devil's Bargain*, out now!

I also want to let you know that, as an incentive from me to you, since you purchased a physical copy of this book, you can send me your name and mailing address via email (carinhartbooks@gmail.com) and I'll mail you a free bookmark and a signed bookplate!

And don't forget to keep reading because I have the cover and a sneak peek at the follow-up book in this series—*The Devil's Bargain*—right now :)

xoxo,

Carin

THE DEVIL'S BARGAIN

A SNEAK PEEK AT THE DEVIL AND HIS BRIDE...

AVA

Red and blue lights suddenly flash into the living room from between the slats in my window.

My hand sloshes as I jump, sending scalding tea onto my thigh. It burns my skin, causing me to yelp as I try to steady both my mug *and* my racing heart.

Eyes dipping to my thigh, Link frowns again. "Are you okay?"

I'm not worried about the burn from the tea. "There's a cop out there."

"I know. You stay here. I'll take care of it."

I'm so freaking glad to hear that. Setting my mug down on the arm of my couch, clasping my fingers together, I offer him a small smile and finally tell him what I'd been meaning to since he rushed over: "Thank you, Link."

To my surprise, his jaw goes tight. "Don't thank me. You haven't asked me what I want for payment yet."

What? Payment?

Of course. Link didn't get to the top of the food chain in Springfield by doing jobs for free, whatever they are. He came because an old girlfriend called him, half-hysterical. That didn't mean that he was doing it out of the kindness of his heart. He wants payment.

I can only imagine how much this is going to cost me.

"I have four thousand in the bank. If I cash out my retirement, that's another ten, I guess. I know that's not much, but—"

"I don't want your money," he says, cutting me off.

Oh. "Then what do you want?"

I don't have much, but my car is pretty decent. My house, too. I have a little jewelry, if that's what he means, or—

"*You*."

The corner of his mouth twitches enough to be noticeable. It's the first sign of amusement I've seen from him since he walked through my door and I tell myself he has to be kidding.

"Me?" I give a tiny laugh of my own. "What do you mean, *me*?"

"It's very simple. I need a wife—"

"And you don't have one already?"

I'm not sure if I sound relieved to hear that, or irrationally pleased. I shouldn't have any reaction at all, but so surprised by the direction this conversation has taken, I give myself away.

Link shakes his head. "That's the problem. As the head of the syndicate, I'm expected to have one. To turn the Sinners into a family, right? Can't do that without a wife, and I've been too busy to find one. And here you are. No husband. No boyfriend," he adds, and I can't help but wonder how he knows *that*, "and no way out of this unless you say yes."

"Link... you can't be serious."

"Dead fucking serious," he agrees.

"Marry you... that's your price. You want me to *marry* you?"

He nods.

Lifting my mug to my lips, I swallow a mouthful of tea. It's still hot and I'm probably scalding the roof of my mouth and the length of my esophagus, but I forced it down. Right now, I need the calm it provides.

"Careful, pet," he says softly. "Easy."

Easy? *Easy?* I've got a dead man—that I *killed*—in my living room, a cop pulled up at my curb, and my former lover-turned-gangster freaking *proposing* to me... and he wants me to take it easy?

That's not what he's doing. Not really. The

275

proposing part, I mean. Link didn't suddenly realize after all these years that he made a mistake and he still loves me.

Oh, no.

I'm just a single woman who is desperate enough to even entertain this insanity.

And I *am*.

"So... if I say yes, it would be a fake marriage. Like a marriage of convenience, one of those in name only. Just so people stop wondering when you'll find a wife... right?"

Link shakes his head. "It'll be real from the moment you say 'I do', pet."

Okay. He must've taken one too many punches to the face when he was younger because I'm beginning to think Link's the crazy one now.

And yet, I can't stop myself from asking, "What would I have to do?"

AVAILABLE NOW

YOU MET BURNS'S ANGEL... NOW MEET THE DEVIL OF SPRINGFIELD AND HIS BRIDE

They say the devil doesn't bargain. I'm here to tell you that he does — but sometimes the price is still way too high.

AVA

I'm in trouble. Deep, deep trouble.

I never meant for it to happen, but my ex is dead—and I'm the one who did it. Whether he deserved it or not... whether anyone will even miss that jerk... it doesn't matter. Joey is dead, and I have to figure out what to do before I get caught with a corpse on my hand.

Enter Lincoln Crewes.

After the way we ended, I swore I would never turn to him again. But we were kids then, and in the fifteen years since I've seen him, he's gone from a scrappy fighter to one of the most powerful men in Springfield's seedy underbelly.

If there's anyone who can help me right now, it's Link. With his power, his money, and his connections, I could put this all behind me.

And all he wants in exchange is my soul... and my hand.

LINK

Ava, Ava, Ava...

She's the one who got away. The reason I've built my entire empire, and the only person I'd burn the whole entire world down for.

I've done things I'm not proud of. They say the road to hell is paved with good intentions, and that's my life story right there. I wanted to show her that I could be the man she wants—the man she deserves—and, by doing so, I became the worst thing for her.

I became the *Devil*.

So I kept my distance, though I always kept my eye on her. If I can't have her, I could at least keep her safe, right?

Wrong. She nearly died, and it's all my damn fault.

When she comes to me, she has no idea that I'm responsible. I'm not about to tell her, either. This is my second chance. My do-over.

Ava is mine again, and no matter what I have to do to keep her, I will. Even force her to marry me in exchange for my protection.

But who will protect her from me?

The Devil's Bargain is the first book in the **Deal with the Devil** series, a collection of interconnected stand-alones set in the fictional crime hotspot of Springfield. It tells the story of the infamous Lincoln Crewes and the one woman he'll do anything possess: Ava Monroe.

Out now!

PRE-ORDER NOW

Don't look out your window—because you might not like what you see...

SIMONE

I can't escape him.

I thought I did. When I slipped off one night, leaving everything in my old life behind, I was ready to sacrifice it all if only to leave *him* behind, too.

But, like always, my ex chases after me. That's what he does, after all. Holding to the vows I was too young and naive to understand, William Burke will have me 'til death do us part.

And then, almost immediately, it does—when Will is slaughtered in a back alley.

He haunts my dreams. Stars in my nightmares. I see him everywhere, hear his voice in my head. I look out my window and he's there. Even dead, I can't escape him...

And that's when I look out my window and realize that it isn't Will watching me from the shadows.

It's another man. A stranger.

A silhouette.

And a *killer*.

Because he's not just watching me. He wants me more than Will did... enough that he'll kill *for* me.

Stalk me.

Take me.

And I want him to...

JAKE

They say the third time's the charm—and whoever they are, they better be right.

I lost Casey. Heather... that was a tragedy.

And now I want Simone.

I refuse to give up on Simone.

So she wears another man's ring. He torments her, and she's in need of a hero.

I can be that for her—I can be *anything* for her—but when she doesn't seem quite that impressed with my gift, I realize I need to get to know my sweet vixen a little better before I make her mine.

And that's exactly what I do. From infiltrating her life to sneaking into her house, I'm here, I'm there, I'm *everywhere*... and she can't escape me.

More importantly, by the time I've done everything I can to convince her there's no one better for her than me, she won't *want* to...

Do you know what's more dangerous than the shadows outside your door?

When he gets tired of watching—and let's himself inside...

**Silhouette is a standalone dark stalker romance that is set in the same universe as *No One Has To Know* and *The Devil's Bargain*.

Releasing on April 23rd — pre-order now!

KEEP IN TOUCH

Stay tuned for what's coming up next! Follow me at any of these places—or sign up for my newsletter—for news, promotions, upcoming releases, and more:

CarinHart.com
Carin's Newsletter
Carin's Signed Book Store

facebook.com/carinhartbooks
amazon.com/author/carinhart
instagram.com/carinhartbooks

ALSO BY CARIN HART

Deal with the Devil series

No One Has To Know *standalone

Silhouette *standalone

The Devil's Bargain

The Devil's Bride *newsletter exclusive

The Devil's Playground

Dragonfly

Dance with the Devil

Ride with the Devil

Reed Twins

Close to Midnight

Really Should Stay